A Dog Called Grk

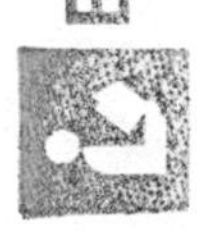

A Dog Called Grk

JOSHUA DODER

Delacorte Press

Published by Delacorte Press
an imprint of Random House Children's Books
a division of Random House, Inc.
New York

This is a work of fiction. Names, characters, places, and incidents either are the product of the author's imagination or are used fictitiously. Any resemblance to actual persons, living or dead, events, or locales is entirely coincidental.

Originally published in the United Kingdom in 2005 by Andersen Press Limited

www.randomhouse.com/kids

Educators and librarians, for a variety of teaching tools,
visit us at www.randomhouse.com/teachers

Library of Congress Cataloging-in-Publication Data
Doder, Joshua.
A dog called Grk / Joshua Doder.
p. cm.
Summary: A British schoolboy finds adventure when he travels to a dangerous foreign country to return a small dog to its rightful owner.
ISBN: 978-0-385-73359-5 (trade)
ISBN: 978-0-385-90374-5 (glb)
[1. Dogs–Fiction. 2. Adventure and adventurers–Fiction.] I. Title.
PZ7.D66295Do 2006
[Fic]–dc22
2006046258

The text of this book is set in 12-point Garamond BE Regular.

Book design by Angela Carlino

Printed in the United States of America

10 9 8 7 6 5 4 3 2 1

First American Edition

A Dog Called Grk

1

One morning in May, the government of Stanislavia issued the following statement:

> **Last night, President Joseph Djinko was arrested. Under questioning, he confessed to forty-seven charges of corruption. Colonel Zinfandel, the Commander-in-Chief of the army and air force of Stanislavia, has assumed control of the country.**

This statement might seem rather short, even a bit boring, but it had amazing consequences throughout the world.

In the White House, the American President's red telephone rang.

In the Elysée Palace, a blue button flashed on the French President's desk.

In 10 Downing Street, an adviser whispered the news into the British Prime Minister's ear.

In 23 Rudolph Gardens, Kensington, London SW7, a tall, handsome man named Gabriel Raffifi ran downstairs to his wife and said, "Quick, darling, get the children! We have to leave!"

When she started to ask what on earth was going on, Gabriel Raffifi replied, "President Djinko has been arrested, and Colonel Zinfandel has taken over the country."

"Oh, my God," said Mrs. Raffifi. She didn't need to ask any more questions. She sprang to her feet, and ran through the house, shouting to her children. "Max? Natascha? Natascha! Max! Where are you?"

If you have never heard of Stanislavia, you needn't feel ashamed. Most people haven't.

Stanislavia is a small, mountainous country in the part of Eastern Europe which is closest to Russia. Its history has been complicated and mostly unpleasant. For centuries, the country was ruled by dictators who imposed their cruel wishes on the miserable population. Fifty years ago, Stanislavia finally achieved independence.

The people of Stanislavia speak a language called Stanislavian. Very few people born outside Stanislavia can speak this language. If you decided to learn it, you would have to devote years of your life to practicing the grammar and vocabulary. Most of the verbs are irregular. Half the idioms make no sense. The dictionary is full of words which are almost impossible to translate into any other language.

"Grk" is one of those words. There isn't one single word in English which means exactly the same as "grk." To translate it, you would need at least three words, and probably more. In a rough translation, "grk" means brave, generous and foolish, all at the same time. You would use the word "grk" to describe a warrior who lost his life in the service of a noble but rather pointless cause.

When Natascha Raffifi was given a tiny puppy by her parents, she thought that he looked very brave, very generous and a tiny bit foolish. So she called him Grk.

2

Every afternoon, Timothy Malt walked home from school along the same route.

Every afternoon, when he got home, he let himself into the house with his own door key. He fetched a carton of orange juice from the fridge, and poured himself a glass. He grabbed three biscuits from the tin, hurried into the sitting room and sat down on the big, squashy sofa. Then he played computer games until his mum came home from her office or his dad came home from his office.

That day, things were different. Tim found a dog.

Actually, the dog found Tim.

During the long afternoons at school, Tim always ignored the teacher's droning voice and dreamed about his computer. After school, he sped home, not wanting to waste any time walking when he could be playing a game.

That day, Tim was hurrying home from school even faster than usual, because he had recently used two months' pocket money to buy a new game. It was a helicopter simulator. He already owned three helicopter simulators for his computer, but this was much more realistic than any of the others. According to the box, pilots used it to practice before flying a new helicopter.

In the past few days, Tim had managed to master most of the basic maneuvers. He could take off. He could fly across fields. He could slalom round tower blocks. Now, he needed to practice flying through the jungle, avoiding the tallest trees, before venturing on his first combat mission.

As Tim hurried along the street towards home, he tried to imagine the best way to fly through the jungle. He waved his hands from right to left as if he was using the control sticks. He imagined all the obstacles that he might encounter. Trees as tall as buildings. Creepers hanging from the branches. Boa constrictors sneaking up the trunks. Parrots flying through the air. Monkeys leaping from tree to tree. He was concentrating so hard on imagining all the jungle's obstacles that he didn't bother looking where he was going, and tripped over a lump of something on the pavement.

The lump yelped.

Tim fell down.

As he fell, Tim stretched out his arms to protect himself. So, his head didn't hit the concrete, but his elbows did. First the right. Then the left. Crunch! Crack! The pain was unbelievable. "Owww," he groaned. He rolled over, clutching his elbows and moaning softly to himself. "Oh, oh, oh. Ohhhh."

After a few seconds of agony, Tim felt something soft touching his cheek. Something soft and wet. He forgot the pain throbbing through his elbows, and opened his eyes.

A pair of little black eyes stared at him. A tiny pink tongue licked his face.

Tim rolled over, and sat up.

The dog wagged its tail.

It was a small dog with beady black eyes. It had white fur with black patches and a perky little tail, which was wagging like a metronome.

Tim wanted to stroke the dog or talk to it, but he knew that he shouldn't. His parents would be furious. His mother loathed dogs. (She was allergic to them.) His father detested dogs. (They made such a lot of noise!) Tim's mother and father had told him never to touch dogs—unless he wanted to catch rabies, fleas and tapeworm.

Tim didn't want a tapeworm slithering through his guts, or fleas crawling under his clothes, or a deadly dose of rabies in his blood. So, he got up, tore his eyes away from the dog and continued walking along the street. As he walked, he rubbed his elbow. It still hurt.

When Tim got to the end of the street, he realized that something was following him. He turned around. There was the dog. Tim said, "Go away. Go back home."

The dog wagged its tail.

Tim said, "Why are you following me? Can you stop following me, please!"

The dog put its head on one side, and stared at him.

Tim bit his fingernail. He always did that when he was

thinking. Then, he took a deep breath, and bellowed, "GO AWAY!"

The dog put its head on the other side, and continued staring at him.

Tim shrugged his shoulders. "Okay. Do what you like." He kept walking along the street. Every few paces, he turned around, and saw that the dog was following him.

After ten minutes, Tim reached his house. He put the key in the lock, then looked down at the dog. "Why are you still here?"

The dog lay down with its head resting on its paws, and looked up at Tim.

Tim looked into the dog's little black eyes, and saw an expression that he recognized. Not sadness. Not loneliness. Not fear. In the dog's little black eyes, Tim saw hunger.

Come to think of it, thought Tim, I'm hungry too.

Tim tried to imagine what would happen if he let the dog into the house. He shook his head. It wasn't worth thinking about. His mother would be so angry that she would stamp her feet and wave her arms above her head. His father would be so angry that he wouldn't say a single word, but his face would go bright red and his eyes would look as if they were going to pop out of his head.

Tim's mother and father were good at being angry. Over the years, they had had a lot of practice.

Tim looked down at the little dog, and said, "Sorry. I can't let you into the house. But I'll go inside, and get some bread. Okay? If you stay here, I'll bring some bread. Do you understand?"

The dog looked at Tim, and seemed to wink one of its

eyes. Tim had the strange feeling that the dog understood exactly what he was saying.

"Good," said Tim. "I'll get the bread, then. You wait here."

Tim turned the key, and opened the door. At that exact moment, the dog sprang forwards, darted between Tim's legs and ran into the house.

"No!" shouted Tim. "No, no, no!"

The dog took no notice. It just kept running.

"Oh, no," groaned Tim. "Mum's going to kill me." He hurried into the house, and shut the door. He took off his coat, and dumped his rucksack in the hall. Then, he started searching for the dog. He knew that he had to remove the dog from the house before his parents came home, or there would be trouble. There would be shouting, and waving arms, and stopped pocket money, and slammed doors, and red faces, and, at the end of it all, Tim would be sent to bed without any supper.

Tim searched from the attic to the basement, checking under every bed, poking his head into every cupboard, and looking anywhere that a dog might hide. But the dog was nowhere to be found.

The clock was ticking. Tim felt a chilly panic in his spine. His mum and dad would be home soon. He fetched a slice of bacon from the fridge, and searched the house again. He held the bacon ahead of him, and called out: "Look, doggie! Bacon! Nice doggie! Come and get the bacon!"

But the dog had disappeared.

Tim poked around the fridge again, and found a pork chop. He held the bacon in one hand and the pork chop in the other. He walked round the house, swinging the meat, shouting and whistling. He opened the cupboards in the kitchen, and thrust the pork chop inside. "Look, doggie! Nice pork chop!" He knelt on the floor in the spare bedroom, peered under the bed and laid the bacon on the carpet. "Look, doggie! Lovely bacon!" Wherever he went, he waved around the bacon and the pork chop, and he shouted, "Yummy, yummy! Free food! Bacon! Pork chop! Come and get it!"

But there was no sign of the dog.

At seven o'clock, Tim was searching the sitting room for the fourteenth time, holding the bacon in one hand and the pork chop in the other, when he heard the sound that he had been dreading for the past two hours: a key turning in the front door. A few seconds later, his mother shouted, "Hi, Tim! I'm home!"

Tim looked down at his hands. The pork chop! The bacon! What could he do with them?

"Tim? Timmy? Are you there?"

"Hi, Mum," called Tim. "I'm in the sitting room." He looked around. The bacon! The pork chop! He had to hide them! But where?

On the sideboard, an ancient Chinese vase sat alongside two gold candlesticks and some family photos in silver frames. The vase was decorated with delicate paintings of blue storks. Tim's father, Mr. Malt, had bought the vase in an auction for fifteen thousand pounds. Mr. Malt loved the vase–although it was difficult to tell whether he loved the delicate paintings of blue storks or the fact that it had cost fifteen thousand pounds. Tim didn't have time to worry about that. He dropped the pork chop inside the vase.

That left the bacon. Tim looked around the room. The sofa! He lifted one of the plump, leather cushions, dropped the bacon, put the cushion on top and sat down.

At that moment, Mrs. Malt walked into the room. "Hello, sweetheart," she said.

"Hi, Mum," said Tim.

Mrs. Malt looked at Tim, who was sitting on the sofa with his arms crossed and a guilty expression on his face. Mrs. Malt said, "What are you doing?"

"Nothing."

"Aren't you playing your new game?"

"I will in a minute."

"Why are you looking so guilty?"

"I'm not."

"Yes, you are," said Mrs. Malt. "What have you done?"

"Nothing, Mum."

"Timothy."

"What?"

Mrs. Malt looked at him for a long time. Then she said, "Are you sure you haven't done anything?"

"Yes, Mum. I'm sure."

"Do you promise?"

"Yes," said Tim. "I promise."

"All right." Mrs. Malt started turning around to go downstairs when she noticed something. At the other end of the sofa, one of the cushions twitched.

Mrs. Malt stared at the cushion with a mixture of horror and astonishment. She had never seen a twitching cushion before. She said, "What's that?"

"What's what?" said Tim, pretending that he hadn't noticed.

"That! That! What is it?" Mrs. Malt pointed at the cushion. It moved. Then, the next cushion moved. As if something was burrowing along the sofa underneath the cushions, getting closer and closer to Tim.

"I don't know," said Tim. "It's probably nothing."

"Nothing?" said Mrs. Malt. "Timothy Malt, do you think I'm a complete idiot?"

"No, Mum."

"Stand up."

"Why?"

"Just stand up!"

"Yes, Mum." Tim stood up.

Mrs. Malt strode over to the sofa, and grabbed the cushion that Tim had been sitting on. She hauled it up, and revealed a dog. A little dog with black eyes, a wagging tail and a slice of raw bacon clasped between its jaws.

"Oh, my God," said Mrs. Malt.

With one quick gulp, the dog swallowed the bacon.

At that moment, at the other end of the house, the front door opened. Mr. Malt had come home from work. He shouted, "Hello! I'm home!"

"Terence!" shouted Mrs. Malt. "Terence! Come here, Terence!"

"Yes, dear," said Mr. Malt. His first name, as you might have guessed, was Terence.

Terence Malt hurried into the sitting room, still wearing his coat and carrying his briefcase. He said, "Hello, Tim. How was school?"

"Fine," said Tim.

"Terence," said Mrs. Malt. "Look!" She pointed at the dog. "What's that?"

Mr. Malt stared for a moment. He blinked. He scratched his nose. Then he said, "It's a dog."

"I know it's a dog," said Mrs. Malt. "But what's it doing here?"

"I've only just got back from work," said Mr. Malt. "How should I know what it's doing here?"

"Well, what are you going to do about it?"

"I'm not exactly sure," said Mr. Malt. "What do you want me to do about it?"

"I want you to get rid of it."

"Then I'll get rid of it," said Mr. Malt. He put his briefcase on the floor, and took a step towards the dog. He said, "Hello, doggie."

The dog wagged its tail.

Mr. Malt took another step towards the dog. "Come here, little doggie." He held out his arms. "Come here."

The dog didn't move.

"Good doggie," said Mr. Malt, and took another step towards the dog. He took another step, and one more, and stretched his arms to grab the dog. Just before Mr. Malt's fingers closed around the dog's neck, the dog ducked, twisted under Mr. Malt's arms and ran to the other side of the room.

Mr. Malt ran one way. Mrs. Malt ran the other way. Tim stood in the middle of the room with a very small smile on his face.

Mr. and Mrs. Malt chased the dog around the room. The dog jumped over the sofa, and wriggled under the chair, and leaped onto the sideboard. Wherever it went, Mr. and Mrs. Malt ran after it with their arms outstretched.

As the dog sprang from the sideboard to the sofa, its tail knocked against the blue Chinese vase.

The vase wobbled.

Mr. Malt stopped running, and stared at the vase. Mrs. Malt stared at the vase. Tim stared at the vase. The dog stared at the vase.

The vase wobbled.

And wobbled.

And wobbled.

And fell over.

Mr. Malt lurched forward, reaching for the vase with both hands, but he was too slow. The vase plummeted onto the floor, and smashed into a hundred pieces.

"Oh, my God," said Mrs. Malt. "What's that?" She pointed.

Lying at the center of all the pieces of shattered vase, there was something pink and white.

"I don't know," said Mr. Malt. He blinked, and stared at the pink and white lump. "It looks like a pork chop."

"A pork chop?"

Before either of them could say another word, the dog leaped forward, took a big bite and sprinted out of the room, carrying the pork chop in its mouth.

Mrs. Malt turned around, and looked at Tim. She said, "For your own sake, Timothy, I hope you have a very, very good explanation for all this."

Tim stared at his mother with his mouth open, but no words came out.

3

Tim was sent to his bedroom with no supper. His pocket money was stopped for a month. His computer was confiscated. He was banned from playing his helicopter simulator game. He sat on his bed, feeling hungry, sad and very sorry for himself.

And the dog?

Mr. Malt searched the whole house, room by room, floor by floor. When he got to the spare bedroom, he found the dog sprawled on the bed, right in the middle of the pink silk duvet, finishing the last scraps of pork chop. Seeing Mr. Malt, the dog licked its lips and wagged its tail. Mr. Malt's face went bright red and his eyes looked as if they would pop out of his head. He shouted, "MELANIE! MELANIE! MEL-LAN-NIE!"

Mrs. Malt's first name, as you might have guessed, was Melanie.

Mrs. Malt came running up the stairs, and charged into the spare bedroom. She was wearing an apron and a pair of long yellow rubber gloves. Mrs. Malt grabbed the dog with both hands. The dog didn't bite her–although it could have done if it had wanted to.

Mrs. Malt walked out of the house, carrying the dog, and threw him into the street. The dog rolled over three or four times, banged into a lamppost and lay on the pavement, not moving. Without giving it another glance, Mrs. Malt went back into the house, and slammed the front door.

4

Once, Tim had flown in a real helicopter. His father's friend David owned a Bell 206 JetRanger. On a Sunday afternoon, they had gone for a ride. That was probably the best day of Tim's life. He had sat in the front, and watched everything that David did. From playing on his computer, Tim was sure that he knew exactly how to fly the helicopter. He tried to persuade David to let him have a go. David had laughed, and said, "Maybe when you're older."

That is one advantage of having parents who work so hard that you never see them: their friends are very rich, so they own cool stuff like helicopters and speedboats. Of course, you never see your parents, because they are always working so hard. You spend more time with your helicopter simulator game than with your mother or your father. But Tim didn't mind. Given the choice, he preferred his helicopter simulator game to his mother or his father.

He lay in bed, and wondered if it would be possible to swap his parents for a new computer.

Actually, he would have been happy to swap them for an old computer.

He had been lying in bed for a long time, but he couldn't sleep. He was depressed, hungry and angry, and thoughts kept spinning round his skull. He thought about the month's pocket money that he wouldn't be getting. He thought about all the time that he wouldn't be able to use his computer, and the helicopter simulator program that he wouldn't be able to play. He thought about his empty stomach, and the fact that he hadn't eaten any supper. He remembered the dog.

I should be angry with the dog, thought Tim. All this is his fault. If it wasn't for him, my belly would be full, and I would have spent the whole night playing my new game.

But, for some reason which he didn't understand, Tim didn't feel at all angry with the dog.

He got out of bed, and walked over to the window. He pushed aside the curtains, and looked out.

Down in the street, he could see the dog. It was lying on the pavement, right in front of the house. It wasn't moving. Tim assumed that the dog was asleep. Then the clouds moved, exposing the moon, which glared down on the street. In the bright moonlight, Tim could see the dog's eyes glinting. Its eyes were open.

Tim lifted his hand, and waved. But the dog didn't react.

5

Mr. Malt worked as an insurance underwriter. Mrs. Malt worked as a financial consultant specializing in corporate takeovers. If you don't know what those words mean, that's okay. I won't explain, because it would only take two or three minutes before my explanations sent you straight to sleep. I'd probably send myself to sleep too.

If their jobs were so boring, why did they spend so much time working on them? The answer is simple: money. Money, money, money. For the huge sums of money that they earned, Mr. and Mrs. Malt wouldn't have minded working twenty-four hours a day. If they could, they would have worked twenty-five.

Every weekday morning, Mr. and Mrs. Malt took turns

to drive Tim to school. That morning, it was Mr. Malt's turn. Mrs. Malt had already gone to work. She liked to arrive in the office earlier than her colleagues, to show them how much harder she worked than anyone else.

Tim and his father left the house. Tim carried his rucksack. Mr. Malt carried his briefcase. They walked along the street to Mr. Malt's Lexus. There, lying on the pavement beside the car, was the dog. It sat up, and wagged its tail. When Tim went to say hello, Mr. Malt snapped, "No time for that. Come on, come on. We have to be at school in exactly eighteen minutes."

"But, Dad," said Tim, who just wanted to pat the dog's head.

"No. Get in the car! We're leaving *right now.*"

They got into the car. The dog sat on the pavement, with its head tipped on one side, watching them. Tim stared through the back window, watching the dog. Mr. Malt started the car, and drove away. They drove down to the end of the street, and joined the main road, where they got stuck behind an old lady in a yellow Ford Fiesta, who was driving extremely slowly. Mr. Malt glanced at the clock on the dashboard. He muttered under his breath, "Come on, come on."

In her yellow Ford Fiesta, the old lady couldn't hear him. Even if Mr. Malt had shouted at the top of his voice, the old lady wouldn't have heard him. She was listening to Beethoven's Second Symphony on the radio, and she had turned the volume to FULL. The old lady hummed to herself, tapped her fingers on the steering wheel and drove at fifteen miles an hour.

"Come on, come on," muttered Mr. Malt. "Do you

think we've got all day?" If there was one thing that Mr. Malt hated, it was being late. If there was another thing that Mr. Malt hated, it was being stuck behind old ladies who drove at exactly half the speed limit.

Tim said, "If he's still there tonight, what will we do?"

"Who? This idiot in the Ford Fiesta?"

"No, Dad. The dog."

"He won't be," said Mr. Malt.

"But what if he is?"

"Then we'll take him to the police. That's what you do with stray dogs."

Tim thought about that for a minute. Then he said, "Wouldn't it be nice to have a dog?"

"No," said Mr. Malt. "It wouldn't." He thrust his foot on the accelerator, and roared past the old lady, leaving her yellow Ford Fiesta in a cloud of black fumes.

6

At school, Tim could not stop thinking about the dog. He sat through his lessons, doodling and daydreaming. He wondered who owned the dog. He tried to imagine what had happened to the dog's owners. Had they lost him? Abandoned him? Forgotten him? Were they searching for him?

Tim had often seen notices pinned to trees in the local park, describing dogs that had been lost, asking for help finding them.

Tim wondered whether he should go to the park, and read all the notices. Perhaps he would find a picture of the little black and white dog, and a note like this:

HAVE YOU SEEN OUR DOG?

She is a small black and white dog with black eyes and a tail that never stops wagging. She is friendly and affectionate. We miss her very much.

We will give a BIG REWARD for her return.

If you find her, or see her, please ring us!

Tim realized that he wouldn't want to find a notice with a picture of the dog. Why not? Because, deep down, he hoped that the dog's owners would never arrive. That way, he might get to keep the dog for himself.

Later in the afternoon, when Tim walked home from school, the dog hadn't moved. It was lying in exactly the same place on the pavement outside Tim's house. When the dog saw Tim, it leaped to its feet, and started wagging its tail.

"Hello, Dog," said Tim. He wished that he knew the dog's name. He felt a bit stupid calling it "Dog." But what else could he call it? He tried to think of a good name. How about Spot? Or Blackie? Or Rover? No, none of those names sounded right. Tim decided that he would just call it Dog. He said, "Okay, Dog. Are you hungry?"

The dog's ears lifted. It was strange: although Tim knew that dogs couldn't understand English, this dog really seemed to know what Tim was saying. "Wait here," said Tim. "I'll fetch you something to eat."

Just like yesterday, he knew he wasn't allowed to bring the dog into the house. Today, he also knew how fast the dog could move. So, before he opened the front door, he turned round to look at Dog. "You stay there. Okay? Don't come into the house. Understand? Otherwise, we'll both get in so much trouble that . . . Well, things will get nasty. Got that?"

In response, the dog just wagged its tail. Nevertheless, Tim had the peculiar sense that the dog understood what he had said.

Tim unlocked the front door, and walked into the house. The dog didn't even try to follow him.

Tim went into the kitchen, opened the fridge and looked at all the food. Then he realized something: he didn't know what dogs eat. Tim had never owned a dog. He had never owned a pet of any sort. He couldn't ask the dog what it wanted to eat; even if the dog *understood* English, it wouldn't *speak* English. What should he do? What should he give the dog to eat? He thought about this for some time, then decided that the answer was simple: he would give the dog exactly what he would have chosen for himself if he hadn't eaten all day.

From the fridge, he took a lump of cheddar cheese, three slices of ham and the jar of Branston Pickle. He found a packet of chocolate biscuits in one cupboard, and a can of lemonade in another. He fetched two slices of white bread from the breadbin, and a packet of Hula Hoops from the kitchen cupboard. He grabbed a spoon and a saucer, put everything on a tray and carried it outside.

The dog was waiting. Tim closed the front door, sat down and spread the dog's meal on the pavement: the bread, the ham, the Hula Hoops, the cheese and the chocolate biscuits, plus a spoonful of Branston Pickle, and some lemonade in a saucer. "There you go, Dog," said Tim. "Eat what you like."

The dog looked at him for a minute, as if it was checking that he was serious. The dog seemed to be saying: "For me? Really? If I eat that, do you promise you won't hit me or kick me or shout at me?"

"I promise," said Tim. He said it aloud, although that made him feel a bit silly; after all, the dog hadn't actually said a single word. Nevertheless, Tim had the feeling that he and the dog understood one another very well. "It's all for you," insisted Tim. "Go on. Eat it."

The dog licked its lips, and started eating. It ate the bread, the ham, the cheese, the Hula Hoops, the chocolate biscuits and the Branston Pickle, then drank the lemonade. When every crumb and drop had gone, the dog walked three times in a circle, lay down on the pavement and looked at Tim with an expression of everlasting gratitude.

"Wait there," said Tim. He hurried into the house, and ran upstairs to his bedroom, where he grabbed a book that he wanted to read. Then he ran downstairs again, and sat on the pavement beside the dog. Tim opened the book, and started reading. The dog closed its eyes, and fell asleep.

At half past seven in the evening, when Mrs. Malt came home from work, she found Tim and the dog sitting on the pavement outside the house. Mrs. Malt said, "What are you doing?"

"Reading," said Tim. He was halfway through the book.

"You shouldn't be sitting here! You'll catch cold."

"Yes, Mum," said Tim.

"Come on, then," said Mrs. Malt. "Come inside."

"Yes, Mum." Tim stood up. "What about Dog?"

"What about it?"

"Can it come inside?"

"No. Of course not."

"Why not?"

"Because we don't have dogs in the house."

"But . . ."

"No buts," said Mrs. Malt. She unlocked the front door, and ushered Tim into the house. Before his mother slammed the door shut, Tim got one last look at the dog, who was standing on the pavement, staring at him with its little black eyes.

That night, because it was Friday, the Malt family ate a take-away together. Every Friday night, Tim was allowed to choose whether they ordered their meal from the Peking Duck, the Taj Mahal or Mario's Special Deep Pan Pizza Parlor. When Mr. Malt came home from work, Mrs. Malt picked up the phone, and said to Tim, "So, what do you want? Chinese? Indian? Italian?"

Tim said, "What do you think the dog would like best?"

Mrs. Malt looked at Mr. Malt, and rolled her eyes.

Mr. Malt said, "Maybe you should choose what you want. Not what the dog would want."

"But I get to choose every Friday," said Tim. "Anyway, I have a nice warm house to sit in, and a nice warm bed to sleep in. The dog doesn't have anything."

"Yes, but dogs are happy with less," said Mrs. Malt.

"How do you know?"

Mrs. Malt couldn't answer that question, because she didn't have a clue what makes dogs happy. So she said,

"That's enough questions. What do you want for supper? If you don't choose, I will."

"Pizza," said Tim. He thought that the dog would probably like pizza more than curry or noodles.

"Good," said Mrs. Malt. She dialed the number on the phone. Immediately, a cheery voice answered. "Buona sera!" (In case you don't know, "buona sera" means "good evening" in Italian.) "This is Mario's Special Deep Pan Pizza Parlor, makers of the best deep pan pizza in all of England. What can I get you, please?"

"A Four Seasons and a Napoletana," said Mrs. Malt.

"You wanna the garlic bread with that?"

"Yes, please. Three, please."

"Three garlic bread, one Four Seasons, one Napoletana. Okey-dokey?"

"Thank you," said Mrs. Malt. "That's perfect."

While Mrs. Malt was ordering the pizza, Mr. Malt sat down at the table with Tim, and had a short but serious conversation with him. "You know we can't keep that dog," said Mr. Malt.

"Why not?"

"Because he doesn't belong to us. Somewhere, his real owners will be looking for him. Imagine you were the owner of that dog. Wouldn't you be sad if someone else kept him?"

"Yes," said Tim. He thought for a moment. "But I'd be even sadder if I knew my dog was sleeping in the street."

"Perhaps he won't sleep in the street tonight," said Mr. Malt. "Perhaps he'll find his own way home."

"What if he doesn't?"

"Let's wait and see."

"Okay," said Tim. "But what if he doesn't? What if he's still there tomorrow? What will we do then?"

"If he is, we'll take him to the police station," said Mr. Malt. "They'll find his owner. Agreed?"

Tim nodded. "Agreed."

Later that night, Tim took a slice of pizza outside. The dog was still sitting on the pavement. Tim knelt beside the dog, and fed it the pizza. When the dog had finished eating, it licked Tim's hand.

Mr. and Mrs. Malt were standing by the window, looking through the glass, watching Tim and the dog. Mrs. Malt said, "What are we going to do?"

Mr. Malt shrugged his shoulders. "It might be fun."

"What do you mean? What might be fun?"

"Having a dog," said Mr. Malt.

"Oh, no," said Mrs. Malt. "Not a chance."

"We could keep it for a week or two. Couldn't we? Until its owners arrive."

Mrs. Malt shook her head. She said, "Terence, do you know how to spell the word 'dog'?"

"Of course I do," said Mr. Malt.

"I'm not so sure you do."

Mr. Malt looked at his wife. Had she gone mad? He said, "There are many things that I don't know, but I do know how to spell 'dog.' "

"Spell it, then."

Mr. Malt shrugged his shoulders. "Yes, dear. You spell 'dog' like this. D. O. G."

"I don't," said Mrs. Malt. "I spell dog like this. D. I. V. O. R. C. E."

Mr. Malt nodded. Now, he understood exactly what his wife was saying. "If the dog's still there in the morning, we'll take it to the police station."

"Thank you, Terence," said Mrs. Malt. She leaned forward, and gave her husband a little kiss on his cheek.

7

In the morning, the dog was still there. It had slept on the pavement outside the house.

Mr. and Mrs. Malt weren't exactly delighted to be spending their Saturday morning driving a stray dog to the local police station, but they had made a promise, and they weren't the type of people who broke their promises. Before leaving, they had a short discussion about which car to take. Mr. Malt thought they should take Mrs. Malt's Volvo. Mrs. Malt insisted that they took Mr. Malt's Lexus. Neither of them wanted the dog's dirty paws mucking up their expensive leather seats. In the end, Mrs. Malt won the argument, as she usually did. Tim climbed into the back of the

Lexus, and held the door open for the dog. "Come on," said Tim. "Get in." The dog jumped into the car, and lay on the backseat, which Mr. Malt had already covered with a thick woolen blanket.

They drove to the local police station, a large redbrick building on the High Street. Mr. Malt parked the car, and the four of them walked into the police station. There was a queue of people waiting to speak to the policeman behind the counter. Every few minutes, the queue shuffled forward. It took a long time. Mr. Malt got more and more impatient. When the Malts finally reached the front of the queue, the policeman tapped his pencil on the counter and said, "Hello. How can I help?"

Mr. Malt replied, "Do you realize we have been waiting for thirty-seven minutes?"

"I'm sorry, sir. We're very busy today. How can I help?"

"Thirty-seven minutes," said Mr. Malt. "It's an absolute disgrace."

"As I said, sir, I'm very sorry. Now, how can I help?"

Tim smiled at the policeman, and said, "It's this dog. I found it. Has anyone reported a lost dog?"

The policeman leaned over the counter, and looked at the dog. "That dog?"

"Yes," said Tim.

The dog wagged its tail, knowing it was the center of attention.

The policeman said, "Who's it belong to?"

"We don't know," said Tim. "If we did, it wouldn't be lost, would it?"

"No need to be clever," said the policeman.

"Sorry," said Tim.

The policeman pointed at the dog. "Does it have a tag? On the collar."

"Dunno," said Tim. He looked at his parents. They both shrugged their shoulders, and admitted that they hadn't bothered looking.

"Maybe you should," said the policeman. He had a little smile on his face, as if he was thinking, Who's being clever now?

Tim knelt on the ground, and had a look. "Yes!" The dog had a little red collar around its neck, and, hanging from the collar, Tim could see a silver tag. Some words had been engraved on the tag.

The policeman said, "What's it say, then?"

Tim leaned forward, and read what was written on the tag. "Nominava Grk. Schl jel trj, jet per flicz da 23 Rudolph Gardens, Kensington, London SW7."

"That doesn't sound like English," said the policeman. "Is there anything on the other side?"

Tim turned over the tag. Engraved on the other side, there were some more words. This time, they were in English. "This must be a translation." He read it aloud. "My name is Grk. If you find me, please return me to 23 Rudolph Gardens, Kensington, London SW7." He looked at the dog. "Is that your name? Grk?"

Hearing its name, the dog wagged its tail furiously and started barking. *Woof woof! Woof woof!*

"Hello, Grk," said Tim.

Woof woof, replied Grk.

Tim looked at his parents. "Now we know its name."

"His name," said the policeman. "That dog is definitely male."

Mrs. Malt was surprised. "How do you know?"

"I have my methods, madam."

"Fascinating," said Mrs. Malt. "Well, Tim, haven't we learned a lot? We know the dog's name. We know he's a he. And we know where he lives. So you'd better say goodbye, because the nice policeman will take him back to his owners."

"That's right," said the policeman. "I'll take him downstairs."

Tim felt terribly disappointed. He wanted to cry. But he was twelve years old, and he knew that boys don't cry. So he gave the dog one last tickle behind its ears. "Goodbye, Grk," he whispered. "Have a nice life."

Grk stuck out his little pink tongue, and licked Tim's hand.

Tim looked at the policeman, wondering about something that he had said. "Why are you going to take him downstairs?"

"That's where the cages are. He'll stay there till we find someone to take him home."

"How long will that be?"

"Not long," said the policeman. "A day or two. Three at the most. As you've already noticed, we're snowed under."

Tim was horrified. Three days! He looked at his parents.

"Oh, no," said Mrs. Malt. "No, no, no. Not a chance."

Ten minutes later, they were driving through the streets of London. On the backseat, Grk laid his head on Tim's leg. Both of them stared out of the window. Every now and then, Tim put his hand on Grk's neck, found the collar and read the address again, just to make sure that he'd got it right. Twenty-three Rudolph Gardens, Kensington, London SW7. It wasn't far, according to the policeman. Twenty minutes' drive. Maybe half an hour, depending on the traffic.

Tim turned over Grk's collar, and looked at the strange writing on the other side. He mouthed the words as he read them: "Nominava Grk. Schl jel trj, jet per flicz da 23 Rudolph Gardens, Kensington, London SW7." What language was that? What kind of people would speak words like those?

Tim tickled Grk behind his ears, then leaned down and whispered to him, "Where are you from, Grk? What language do you speak?"

Grk did not reply.

8

Corporal Danko Pinot joined the Stanislavian Army when he was eighteen. See the world, they had said. Experience adventure, they had said. Travel, they had said. But he didn't. He just saw the inside of one barracks, then the inside of another.

When he was posted to London, he thought that things would improve. At last, he thought, he'd get to see the world. But he didn't. He saw the front of the Stanislavian Embassy in Kensington, which was where he had to stand for twelve hours every day, wearing a black uniform and a peaked cap. His job was frightening away burglars and terrorists, but there were never any burglars or terrorists to frighten away. He mostly read the paper. He got to know the postman, the milkman, the cleaning-ladies and the other guards who worked in the other big houses that lined Rudolph Gardens.

When the Raffifi family lived in the house, things had been better. The Raffifis were friendly, and they had two great kids, Natascha and Max. The Ambassador, Gabriel Raffifi, always remembered the birthdays of his guards, and sent a crate of beer as a present. Mrs. Raffifi made friends with the guards' wives, who were even more bored in London than their husbands, and even more depressed by English food and English weather. In the mornings, when Max and Natascha hurried out of the house, late for school as usual, they always had time to say something nice to the guards.

Two weeks ago, the regime had changed in Stanislavia. The Raffifi family had been arrested by the Secret Service. When that happened, Corporal Pinot didn't say anything to anyone, not even his wife. If you worked for the army, your job was simple: you kept your mouth shut and protected the interests of your country. You weren't paid to have opinions about who was running the country, or who should be running the country.

But he couldn't help feeling sorry for the Raffifi family. They had been such nice people. Specially the kids. When they were arrested, he had known that his job was going to get worse. The next Stanislavian Ambassador wouldn't deliver a crate of beer on Corporal Pinot's birthday. The next Stanislavian Ambassador's wife wouldn't make friends with Corporal Pinot's wife. If the next Stanislavian

Ambassador had children, they wouldn't be as charming and friendly as Max and Natascha Raffifi, and they certainly wouldn't have a cute little dog like Grk.

Now, you're probably wondering why I have told you about Corporal Pinot. What does he have to do with the story? Why does it matter what he thought about his job, or the Raffifis, or anything else?

Well, if you didn't understand Corporal Pinot, you wouldn't understand what happened next. And if you didn't understand what happened next, then nothing would make sense at all.

It was a Saturday morning, a few days after the Raffifi family had been arrested and removed from the Stanislavian Embassy. As he did every day, Corporal Pinot was standing outside the Embassy, looking up and down the street, keeping his eyes open, checking for suspicious characters.

Rudolph Gardens was a short street. Outside most of the huge white houses, a flag flapped on the end of a tall pole, and one or two uniformed security guards watched the street. Corporal Pinot knew most of them. On Monday evenings, he watched the football with Olaf and Sven from the Swedish Embassy. Every weekend, he would share some chips and a glass of beer with Pierre, the guard at the Belgian Embassy. Once, he had played poker with Raphael and Bobby from the Argentinian Embassy, but they won so much of his money that he never went back.

A car cruised slowly down the street, and rolled to a halt outside the Stanislavian Embassy.

Corporal Pinot stared at the car. Through the windscreen, he could see a man and a woman in the front, and a little boy in the back. They didn't look like terrorists or burglars, but Corporal Pinot had been taught to be suspicious of everyone. Like the teachers used to say at military school: "If you're prepared for the worst, then you'll usually be pleasantly surprised." Corporal Pinot walked over to the car, and tapped on the driver's window.

Inside the car, the driver pressed a button, and the window slid open. The driver said, "Good morning."

Corporal Pinot said, "No parking." He spoke English with a strong foreign accent, and his grammar was occasionally inaccurate. "It is forbidden."

"We won't be long," said the driver. "We have to see someone."

"About what?"

"We've found a dog. A lost dog. This is the address on his collar." The driver pointed at 23 Rudolph Gardens.

"A dog? What dog?"

At that moment, the young boy leaned forward between the front seats, and said, "His name is Grk."

Corporal Pinot said, "Grk?"

"Yes," said the boy. "Grk."

"You have found Grk?"

"Yes. Why? Do you know him?"

"Of course I know him. He is very good dog."

"Who does he belong to?"

Before answering that question, Corporal Pinot straightened up, and looked around. He wanted to check that no one was watching, and no one could hear what he was saying. Then he leaned down again, peered through the window, and spoke in a whisper. "Take him away from this place, please."

The boy was surprised. "Why?"

"If he stays, he will be killed."

Now all three of the Malts were surprised. (As you will have guessed already, the car's occupants were Mr. Malt, Mrs. Malt, Tim and Grk.) Mr. Malt said, "Killed? Who would kill him?"

"I cannot say you," replied Corporal Pinot.

"This is ridiculous," blurted Mr. Malt. "Who could possibly want to kill a little dog?"

Corporal Pinot whispered, "Okay, okay. I say you. Grk was belonging to daughter of man who lived here. She was little girl. About your age." As Corporal Pinot said those words, he looked at Tim. "Yes, yes, your age. Her name was Natascha."

As soon as Corporal Pinot spoke Natascha's name, there was a loud barking from the backseat. *Woof woof! Woof woof!* Grk was so excited to hear his owner's name that he couldn't help leaping up and down on the seat, frantically wagging his tail. He turned his head from side to side, looking out of the car's windows, hoping to see her. He barked loudly. *Woof woof! Woof woof!* His barks seemed to be saying, "I'm here! I'm here!"

But there was no answer. Natascha didn't come running to find him, as she usually did when he barked. Grk looked puzzled. He barked again. *Woof woof? Woof woof?* This time, his barks seemed to be saying, "Where are you? Where are you?"

Hearing the loud barks, Corporal Pinot looked terrified. "You must take him away. Please."

Tim said, "But where is she? The girl who owns him?"

"I cannot say you," replied Corporal Pinot. "I will have big trouble."

"From who?" asked Mr. Malt.

"From my boss. From my government."

Mr. Malt opened his mouth. Before Mr. Malt could speak another word, Corporal Pinot straightened up. Out of the corner of his eye, he had seen some movement behind him. Corporal Pinot rapped his knuckles against the windscreen, and said, "Move along, please. Move along."

Mr. Malt was very puzzled, but he did as he was asked. He revved the engine, and accelerated down Rudolph Gardens.

Corporal Pinot stood there, watching the car, until he realized that someone was standing beside him. He turned around, and saw the new Ambassador, who had recently arrived from Stanislavia. Immediately, Corporal Pinot saluted. "Good morning, sir!"

"Good morning, Corporal," replied the Ambassador. "Who was that? In the car?"

"Some tourists," replied Corporal Pinot. "They were lost. They asked the way to Buckingham Palace."

"Did you tell them the way?"

"Yes, sir."

"Excellent." The Ambassador nodded. "Keep up the good work."

"Yes, sir," said Corporal Pinot, and he saluted again.

9

When the Malt family got back to their house, Tim sat on the pavement with Grk for ten minutes, stroking his head and gazing into his soft, black eyes. "I'm sorry," whispered Tim. "They won't let you come inside. But I'll get you some bread. And a bowl of water. Would you like that?"

Grk blinked his beady eyes, put his head on one side and thumped his tail against the pavement. Tim took that to mean yes. So he went inside and fetched a slice of bread, a piece of bacon and a bowl of water. He brought them outside, and gave them to Grk, who ate the bacon in one gulp and the bread in another, then started lapping the water.

"Come inside," said Mr. Malt to Tim. "It's lunchtime. And, before you ask, the answer is no."

But Tim wasn't even going to bother asking. Leaving Grk outside, he followed his father into the house.

Mr. Malt shut the front door, and said, "I've remembered something about the girl who owns that dog. What did the guard say her name was?"

"Natascha," said Tim.

"That's right. Natascha. Well, I think she must have been the daughter of the ambassador. They lived in the embassy. I read about it in the *Telegraph*. They come from some country with a funny name, and the political situation has changed. They must have been recalled home. That's what happens if you're an ambassador."

Tim thought about what his father had said. It didn't make sense. "Why would they leave their dog behind?"

"Perhaps they didn't like their dog. Perhaps they wanted to go home without it."

"Him," said Tim.

"Sorry. Him. Perhaps they wanted to go home without him."

Tim shook his head. It didn't sound right. If you spent any time with Grk, you knew that his owners couldn't possibly be horrible. Horrible people have horrible dogs. Grk was affectionate, honest and gentle. Therefore, his owners must be affectionate, honest and gentle–and not the type of people to dump their dog in the street.

"Come on," said Mr. Malt. "We'll look on the Internet."

They trudged upstairs to Mr. Malt's study, which was a small room in the attic with a desk, a fax machine, a computer and a telephone. When Mr. Malt worked at the weekend–which he usually did–he locked himself in this windowless room. During the summer, the air grew stale and stuffy, but Mr. Malt didn't mind. Even when the sun was shining, he preferred to sit in his study, staring at his computer. That explained why he was so rich. But it also explained why his skin was so pale, and why he made such a horrible wheezing noise when he climbed the stairs.

Anyway, that's enough about Mr. Malt's health. It's his problem, not ours. His computer is all that matters to us. Tim and Mr. Malt climbed the stairs to the top of the house, and went into the study. Mr. Malt sat down at his desk, switched on the computer and connected to the Internet. He typed some phrases into a search engine, and pressed ENTER. Mr. Malt had a super-fast connection to the Internet, because he didn't like waiting for things. He liked things to happen *right now.* After two seconds, he said, "There you go. That's the owner of the dog." He pointed at the screen.

On the BBC's Web site, Mr. Malt found a page from last week's news. In a country called Stanislavia, the government had changed. The President had been arrested, and the Commander-in-Chief of the army and air force had taken control. All around the world, the ambassadors of Stanislavia had been called home. Mr. Malt swung round in his swively chair and smiled at his son. "Well, that's that."

Tim said, "What's what?"

"That explains why the dog has been wandering the streets of London. Its owners are hundreds of miles away. They've gone home to their own country. What's it called again?" Mr. Malt peered at the screen. "That's right. Stanislavia. Strange word, isn't it?"

Tim didn't answer. He was thinking about Grk, and wondering whether the poor little dog would ever see his owners again. Grk seemed like such a nice dog. His owners must be good people. They wouldn't leave him behind unless they had to. Tim said, "Where is Stanislavia?"

"A long way away from here," replied Mr. Malt.

"Where?"

"Near Russia."

"But where?"

"That's enough," said Mr. Malt. "Stop pestering me with questions." He turned around and stared at his computer, as if Tim wasn't even in the room.

Actually, Mr. Malt didn't have a clue where Stanislavia was. But he wasn't going to admit that. Mr. Malt never liked admitting that he didn't know the answer to a question.

The rest of that day was like a normal Saturday for Tim: his dad sat upstairs, doing some work, and his mum sat downstairs, doing some work, and Tim wandered around the house, feeling bored. He read a book, and watched a bit of TV. Sometimes, he thought that his life would be more interesting if he had some brothers and sisters. At least he would have someone to talk to.

A year or two ago, he had asked his mother why he didn't have any brothers or sisters. She had replied, "Because one child is quite enough trouble."

After that, Tim didn't ask any more questions.

In the evening, the Malt family ate supper together. They had pork chops and mashed potato, followed by vanilla ice cream (for Tim), a slice of chocolate cake (for Mr. Malt) and an apple (for Mrs. Malt, who had to watch her weight).

During supper, Mr. Malt cleared his throat and said, "Tim, your mother and I have reached a decision. We've decided what to do about the dog. Tomorrow morning, we'll take him to Battersea."

"Battersea?" Tim knew that Battersea was on the other side of London, but he couldn't imagine why Grk would want to go there. "Why? What happens in Battersea?"

"Haven't you ever heard of Battersea Dogs' Home?"

"Yes," said Tim. "I think so."

"They look after lost dogs. If you find a dog, you take it to Battersea Dogs' Home, and they'll find its owner."

Tim thought for a minute. Then he said, "Couldn't we look after Grk?"

"No," said Mr. Malt.

"Why not?"

"You know your mother's allergic to dogs."

"But she didn't sneeze when Grk was in the car."

"That's not the point," said Mr. Malt.

"Then what is the point?"

"The point is," said Mr. Malt. "The point is . . . The point is . . ." He looked at his wife, hoping that she might know what the point was.

She did. "The point is, Tim, it's your bedtime."

"Oh, Mum."

"No moaning. Time for bed. And don't forget to clean your teeth."

"But . . ."

"No buts. Bed."

Tim pushed back his chair, slouched out of the room and trudged upstairs to bed. Mr. and Mrs. Malt sat downstairs, reading some papers for work. At ten o'clock, they would watch the news. Then, they would go to bed too.

On his way from the bathroom to his bedroom, Tim stopped by the window, and looked through the glass. He could see the street below. He blinked, and tried to focus his eyes to see clearly in the darkness. Yes! Yes, there! Down on the pavement! A small blob of black and white. It was Grk, curled on the paving stone, sleeping outside the house.

Tim went into his bedroom, and changed into his pajamas. He climbed into bed, lay under the duvet and wondered about the family who had owned Grk. He thought about the girl. What was her name? What had the guard called her? Tim thought for a long time; then he remembered. Natascha! That was it. Natascha. The guard had said that she was about the same age as Tim. He wondered how she had felt, leaving her dog behind.

At that moment, Tim realized what he had to do. He had to go downstairs, and persuade his parents to contact Grk's owners. It was their duty. They had to tell Natascha that they had found her dog. If they didn't do that, they were no better than criminals.

Tim knew the difference between right and wrong. He knew that stealing was wrong. He also knew that finding something, but not giving it back, is no better than stealing.

He got out of bed, grabbed his dressing gown, and pulled it on over his pajamas. He left his bedroom, and tiptoed downstairs. He knew that if his parents heard him on the stairs, they would order him back to bed without even listening to him.

If he had thought about what he was doing, he wouldn't have gone downstairs at all. He would have waited until the morning. But Tim wasn't specially good at thinking before he did things. He was passionate and impulsive. So he tiptoed downstairs to the sitting room, pushed open the door and hurried inside. His parents looked up. Quickly, Tim said, "I've been thinking, and I've realized what we have to do. We have to find the people who own Grk. The girl, Natascha. And her father, the Ambassador. We can't take him to a dogs' home. It's just not fair." His words came out in a rush, and, when he'd finished speaking, he just stood there, waiting for his parents to reply.

Mr. and Mrs. Malt looked at one another, as if they were deciding which of them should reply. Somehow, without speaking, they made the decision. Mr. Malt said, "I'm sorry, Tim, but that's just not possible. We can't take him abroad. Battersea Dogs' Home has an excellent reputation. They'll find him a new home."

"What if they don't?"

"Well, they will."

"But what if they don't? What happens then?"

Mr. Malt looked solemn. "We'll cross that bridge when we come to it."

"They'll put him to sleep," said Tim. "Won't they? That's what they do to lost dogs."

"He's a very sweet little dog," said Mr. Malt. "Someone is sure to want him."

"But if they don't, he'll be put to sleep. Won't he?"

Neither Mr. nor Mrs. Malt said another word.

Tim shook his head. "We can't let them do that."

"Time for bed," said Mrs. Malt. "We'll talk about this in the morning."

"No," said Tim. "Let's talk about it now. We've got to find his owners."

"Tim . . ."

"We've got to!"

"All right," said Mrs. Malt. "Tomorrow, we'll take him to Battersea. Then, we'll phone his owners. If they want him, they can come and fetch him from Battersea. How does that sound?"

"That sounds terrible," said Tim. "His owners are hundreds of miles away. Aren't they, Dad?"

Mr. Malt glanced at his wife, shrugged his shoulders and nodded.

"You see?" said Tim. "You can't take him to Battersea. You'll be murdering him!"

"Sorry, Tim," said Mr. Malt. "But there's nothing else we could do."

"We could keep him."

Mr. Malt shook his head. "That simply isn't possible. You know your mother is allergic to dogs."

"No, she's not," said Tim. "She just pretends to be."

"Bed," said Mr. Malt. He pointed at the door.

"But . . ."

"No buts," said Mrs. Malt. "Bed. Now."

"You're both horrible," shouted Tim. "I hate you!"

"You don't mean that," said Mrs. Malt. "Now, go to bed."

"Good night," said Mr. Malt. "See you in the morning."

Tim looked at his parents. In a quiet voice, he said, "I

hate you." Then he walked out. He thought about slamming the door, but decided not to. That would have been childish. He closed the door quietly and padded upstairs.

When Tim had gone, Mr. Malt looked at Mrs. Malt, and said, "He seems terribly upset."

"He'll get over it," said Mrs. Malt.

"Maybe we should think about keeping the dog," said Mr. Malt. "Just for a couple of days."

Mrs. Malt stared at her husband. "You seem to have forgotten two things, Terence."

"Oh, yes? What have I forgotten?"

"Firstly, I'm allergic to dogs. Secondly, your vase."

"My vase," repeated Mr. Malt. "Oh, yes. My vase." He remembered how much the vase had cost. He remembered how much he had loved those delicate paintings of blue storks. And he remembered the current location of his vase: smashed into a hundred pieces and stuffed in a brown envelope, waiting to be taken to the repairman for Chinese vases. "Maybe you're right. Maybe we should take the dog straight to Battersea."

"Of course I'm right," said Mrs. Malt. "Am I ever wrong?"

"No, dear. Never."

Upstairs, Tim knew what he was supposed to do: he was supposed to climb into bed, read his book until he felt tired, then go to sleep. But he didn't do any of those things. Instead, he sneaked up another flight of stairs to the attic, tiptoed into his father's study and pulled the big *Atlas of the World* out of the bookshelf. He put the atlas on the table, and looked for Stanislavia in the index. How was it spelled? Stan . . . Stanis . . . Something like that. He looked up Stan in the index. After Standish, Stanford, Stanger and Stanhope, he found Stanislavia. The index had this entry: Stanislavia 37/B3.

Tim understood what that meant. On page 37 of the atlas, there would be a square numbered B3, where he would find Stanislavia.

And he did.

According to the atlas, Stanislavia was a small country surrounded by mountains. It had no borders with the sea, although a long, thin lake ran down its middle.

Tim turned over the pages, and found a map of Europe. On the left-hand side of the map, he found Britain. On the right-hand side of the map, he found Stanislavia. Anyone wishing to travel between the two countries would have to cross the English Channel, lots of mountains and several countries.

It was a long way from London to Vilnetto, the capital of Stanislavia. A long, long way. Even so, Tim knew what he had to do.

Tim tiptoed downstairs, and returned to his bedroom. He found his alarm clock, and set the alarm for four o'clock in the morning. Then, he put the clock under his pillow, so it would wake him but not his parents. He switched off the light, closed his eyes and drifted into a dreamy sleep.

He was woken by the bleeping of his alarm. For a moment, he thought that he was still dreaming. Then, he remembered what he had decided to do. He slid out of bed, and pulled on some clean clothes. He chose warm, sensible clothes: his favorite jeans, a pair of thick socks, a blue T-shirt and a thick red wooly jumper.

He slid open the door of his bedroom. It creaked. He waited for a minute, but the house was quiet. The creak hadn't woken his parents. He tiptoed out of the room, and padded downstairs to the hallway, where the family's coats were hanging from a line of hooks. Tim reached into his father's jacket. In one of the pockets, he found what he was looking for: his father's wallet. He opened it. He removed all the cash–ninety-five pounds–and a credit card. Then he slid the wallet back into the jacket.

He tiptoed upstairs, past his parents' bedroom, and climbed to the top of the house. In the attic, he switched on his father's computer, and connected to the Internet. He found the travel site where his father always booked tickets. Tim had never bought tickets before, but he'd often seen his father buying books and CDs on the Internet, and it was very easy: you just typed the credit card number, and the tickets were yours.

With his father's credit card, Tim bought two tickets from London to Vilnetto, the capital of Stanislavia. The flight left at ten past seven. Tim looked at the clock on the screen. It was quarter past four. He needed to go now. According to the site, the tickets would be waiting for him at the airport.

He clicked another part of the screen, and summoned the calculator. Using it, he did a quick sum. He added ninety-five pounds to the price of the tickets, then divided the sum by the amount of his weekly pocket money. The answer was one hundred and eighty-three. He grabbed a pen and some paper, and wrote a quick note to his parents.

Dear Mum and Dad,

I have gone to Stanislavia to return Grk to his owners. I will be back when I have found them. Sorry about taking the money, but I need it. Please debit my pocket money for the next 183 weeks.

Love from

Tim

He put the note on the keyboard, where his father would be sure to see it. Then, he switched off the computer, and tiptoed down the stairs. As he went past his parents' room, he paused and listened. There was no noise. They were comfortably asleep.

Downstairs, Tim collected a few more things. In the right-hand drawer of his mother's desk, he found his passport. In the left-hand drawer, he found a ball of string, and he cut a good length from it. He fetched his coat from the hall, then walked out of the house, and closed the front door behind him. The lock clicked.

He looked up and down the street. It was empty.

Tim thought: Empty?

Then he thought: Empty???!!!

Tim realized that he'd been a complete idiot. He hadn't even checked that Grk was still sleeping outside the house. If Grk had gone, his preparations were useless.

He whistled. He was careful to whistle very quietly, because he didn't want to wake any of the neighbors. If they saw him standing in the street at half past four in the morning, they would ring his parents straightaway. But he whistled so quietly that Grk couldn't hear him either. So he whistled a little bit louder. Then he whispered: "Grk! Grk! Where are you?"

There was no sign of the dog. What if Grk had gone? Maybe he had found a warmer, cozier place to spend the night.

Tim stopped whispering, and spoke in a normal tone of voice. "Grk! Grk! Come here!"

A little white head poked out from under the nearest car. A pair of soft black eyes stared at Tim.

"Good boy," whispered Tim. "Come here!"

Grk wriggled out from under the car, and sprinted towards Tim, wagging his tail.

Tim said, "Do you want to go home? Do you want to see Natascha?"

Maybe Tim was imagining things, but he thought that, at the sound of those words, Grk's tail wagged even more furiously.

Tim leaned down. He found the red collar fastened around Grk's neck. He reached into his pocket, grabbed the string and tied one end onto the collar. Holding the other end, he stood up. "Okay. Let's go."

Together, Tim and Grk started walking along the street, away from Tim's house, and towards . . . Towards what? Towards the end of their journey, wherever that might be.

10

Timothy Malt knew that his dad often went on business trips to Europe, which meant leaving the house at six o'clock in the morning and catching a taxi to the airport. So, that's what Tim decided to do.

Tim walked down to the end of his street, turned left, then right, and headed towards the main road. In his hand, he was holding a piece of string, which was tied to Grk's red collar. Grk trotted beside him, sniffing the air.

When they reached the main road, Tim was suddenly very scared. He looked at the cars and the lorries. He saw all the strangers. He had an unnerving sense of the world's vast size, and how small he was. He wondered whether it would be better to turn around, and go home.

Then he looked down at Grk. Although he knew the dog wouldn't reply, he asked him a question. "Shall we go back home?"

The little dog looked up at Tim, blinked his soft, black eyes and yapped. *Woof!*

What did he mean by that?

I don't know. Nor did Tim.

If you could understand what a dog said, you'd learn some pretty interesting things. Unfortunately, dogs speak Dog and humans speak Human and there's no one on earth who can speak both.

So Tim had to decide for himself. Should they go onwards? Or scurry home? He didn't even need to think about it. He took a firm grip of the string in his hand, and walked along the main road to the traffic lights. Tim and Grk stood by the lights for five minutes, waiting for a taxi. One went past. Another did too, taking no notice of Tim, although he was frantically waving his arm. The third taxi stopped.

Tim stood on tiptoes, leaned through the window and looked at the driver. "Heathrow Airport, please," said Tim.

"Heathrow? Yeah, all right," said the driver. "Hop in."

Tim opened the door, and ushered Grk into the taxi.

The driver turned around, and wagged his finger. "Hey, hey, hey. No dogs."

"Why not?"

"No smoking, no ice cream, no dogs. That's the rules."

Tim said, "He's a very clean dog."

"Rules is rules. No smoking, no ice cream, no dogs. Sorry."

"He'll sit on the floor. He won't make a mess, I promise."

"My cab, my rules," said the driver. "Sorry." He glanced into the mirror, and prepared to drive away.

"Wait," said Tim. "What if I pay an extra ten pounds?"

The driver stared at him for a minute. "Twenty."

Tim nodded.

"Go on, then," said the driver. "Rules are made to be broken, right?"

Tim stepped into the taxi, slammed the door and slumped onto the backseat. Grk lay on the floor between his feet. The driver glanced at Tim in the rearview mirror. "Heathrow, you said?"

"Yes, please."

"Coming right up." The driver started his engine, and accelerated into the traffic.

The drive to Heathrow took nearly an hour. The driver chattered nonstop, but Tim ignored him. He was wondering what would happen later in the day. What would he do when he arrived in Stanislavia? What kind of place would it be? Big? Small? Crowded? Empty? Wet? Dry? Hot as a desert? Cold as the North Pole?

What about Grk's owners? What if he couldn't find them? He didn't even know their names. He just knew that they had a daughter called Natascha, who was about the same age as him. What if his dad was right, and they did hate their dog? What if they had deliberately dumped Grk in London? What if . . . ? What if . . . ? What if . . . ?

As these thoughts spun around Tim's head, he felt more and more frightened. His heart started beating faster.

He wondered if he was doing something terrible. Would his parents disown him? Would he get thrown in a children's home? Would he be locked in prison? Would he ever come back from Stanislavia?

He looked out of the window, and wondered whether this would be the last time that he ever saw the streets of London.

At Heathrow Airport, Tim had to give sixty-three pounds to the taxi driver. More than half his money had gone, and he hadn't even left Britain.

The driver pocketed the cash, and grinned. "Have a nice holiday, mate."

"I'm not going on holiday," said Tim.

"Where are you going?"

Tim was tempted to reply, "That's none of your business." However, he knew it was rude to say that, even to a greedy man who had recently taken more than half your money. "I'm going on a business trip."

"Bit young for business, aren't you?"

"No."

"Well, I hope it's profitable. Good luck, mate." The driver gave a thumbs-up, and drove away.

Tim and Grk walked into the airport. By the door, they were stopped by two tall policemen, who were wearing bulletproof vests and carrying machine guns.

The first policeman had a little mustache, which looked like a black slug hanging on to his lip. He pointed at Grk. "You can't bring him in here, sir."

"Why not?"

"No dogs in the airport," said the second policeman.

He was clean-shaven, but he had big, bushy eyebrows which looked like a pair of black slugs clinging to the top of his head.

Tim wanted to giggle (all those slugs looked very funny), but he knew that policemen get upset if you laugh at them. So he said, "I have to take the dog into the airport. He's flying on the plane with me."

The two policemen looked at one another. The first policeman said, "We can't let him in. The rules say, no dogs in the airport."

The second policeman shook his head. "But the rules also say, allow passengers into the airport."

"If he's a dog, we can't let him into the airport."

"But if he's a passenger, we have to let him into the airport."

The two policemen stared at one another. Neither of them knew what to do.

The first policeman said, "We're in a bit of a pickle."

"We certainly are," said the second policeman.

Tim looked at his watch. His flight was due to leave in one hour and fifty minutes. On the Web site, the instructions had specifically said that he had to check in two hours before departure. "I have to check in now. Otherwise, the plane will take off without me."

"Don't worry," said the first policeman. "The plane won't leave without you."

The second policeman added, "Give us a moment to unpickle ourselves."

The two policemen retreated a few feet, so Tim couldn't hear what they were saying, and conferred in whispers. After a couple of minutes of intense discussion, they both nodded. When they returned to Tim, their sluggy faces beamed with big smiles. "Come this way, young man," said the first policeman. "And bring the dog."

"You've got an official escort," explained the second policeman.

If they walked through the airport with Tim, they had decided, then he would be allowed to bring the dog inside. After all, what could a dog do wrong when accompanied by two armed policemen? Together, the four of them walked through the airport, and found the check-in desk for AIR STANISLAVIA, also known as AS. Tim produced his passport and his father's credit card, and handed them to a tall, slim woman with brown hair sitting behind the counter. "I've come to collect my tickets," said Tim.

The woman took his passport and the credit card. She glanced at the two big policemen who were standing on either side of Tim. I understand, she thought. I know what's going on. He must be a Very Important Person. That's why he's accompanied by two policemen. She decided to be very polite to this very important person. She said, "Thank you, sir. Two tickets. Is that right?"

"Yes," said Tim. He liked being called sir.

"One ticket is for you?"

"Yes."

"And who will be using the second ticket?"

"Him." Tim pointed at the floor.

The woman leaned over her counter, and looked at Grk. If Tim hadn't been a VIP, she might have asked some questions. Like "Why does your dog get a seat to himself?" Or "What's a boy like you doing all alone?" Or even "Is this really your credit card?" However, she knew that a VIP should never be bothered with such questions. Instead, she said, "I've upgraded you to First Class. I hope you'll be comfortable there, sir."

"Thanks," said Tim.

Grk wagged his tail. Perhaps he was already daydreaming about the superior quality of food served in First Class.

The two policemen glanced at one another. One of them raised his sluggy eyebrows. The other smiled, and his sluggy mustache lifted at the corners of his mouth. They realized that this little boy must be a Very Important Person. Only VIPs get upgraded to First Class.

The woman behind the counter looked at Tim and said, "Do you have any luggage, sir?"

"No," said Tim.

The stewardess and the two policemen were impressed. Only very rich people can afford to travel without luggage; they buy what they need when they get there. The stewardess smiled. "Here's your boarding card and your passport. Have a nice flight."

The two policemen escorted Tim and Grk through the airport, making sure that he always went straight to the front of every queue. The woman behind the counter at AS had telephoned to her colleagues on the airplane, warning them to expect a VIP. When Tim and Grk arrived, accompanied by the two policemen, all the other passengers stared at them, and started whispering. "That's Prince George," whispered one of them. "He's the King of Denmark's grandson."

"No, no," whispered another passenger. "It's Davy Nickers, the singer with that new boy band."

"You're both wrong," insisted a third passenger. "That's Gary Grant. He's only fifteen, and he's already on fifty grand a week with Manchester United."

Luckily, Tim couldn't hear any of the passengers, or he would have started giggling.

He said goodbye to the two policeman, who shook his hand, and wished him a good flight. Then, one of the air stewardesses led Tim and Grk onto the plane.

At the same time that Tim and Grk were settling into their seats, a couple of other important things were happening.

Firstly, the woman behind the counter at AS was ringing her boss in Vilnetto, the capital of Stanislavia. She warned him that a Very Important Person would be arriving on the flight from London.

Secondly, Mr. and Mrs. Malt were waking up.

Just like every other morning, they lay in bed for ten minutes, listening to the radio. Then, they got up. Mr. Malt had a bath and Mrs. Malt had a shower. (They had two bathrooms, because they didn't like seeing one another with no clothes on.) They went downstairs, and ate some breakfast. After five minutes, Mrs. Malt stood by the stairs and shouted, "Tim! Tim! It's time to get up!" There was no answer. She sighed, shook her head, climbed the stairs and went to wake up her son.

Mr. Malt stayed in the kitchen, eating a bowl of bran flakes with dried bananas, drinking a cup of black coffee and reading the *Sunday Telegraph.* He read an extraordinary story about the migratory patterns of Canada geese. It was so fascinating that he didn't bother looking up when his wife came back into the room, and said, "Terence!"

"Yes, dear?"

"Oh, Terence! You're not going to believe what's happened!"

"Yes, dear," said Mr. Malt, and continued reading about Canada geese.

"Oh, my God," said Mrs. Malt. "What are we going to do?"

"Yes, dear."

"Terence. Are you listening to me?"

"Yes, dear," said Mr. Malt, although he didn't look up from the *Telegraph.* "What seems to be the problem?"

Mrs. Malt took a deep breath. "Tim isn't in his bedroom. I think he's been kidnapped."

"Really, dear?" Mr. Malt nodded, and he read another couple of sentences about Canada geese. Then, he realized what his wife had said. He lifted his eyes from the newspaper, and glared at her with a confused expression. "*Kidnapped?* Did you say *kidnapped*?"

11

If you are going to understand this story properly, there are a few things that I should explain. I should tell you about Grk's owners, and the country that they came from, and the political situation there.

In order to do that, we must go back in time.

A few days before Tim found Grk in the street (or, depending on your point of view, Grk found Tim), the President of Stanislavia was arrested. He was taken to prison, and guarded by fifty soldiers. The Commander-in-Chief of the army and air force of Stanislavia, Colonel Zinfandel, took control of the country.

• • •

For most of his life, Gabriel Raffifi had worked for the Government of Stanislavia. He served in the diplomatic service. He earned a reputation as a man who would be willing to sacrifice his own life for truth, justice and the dignity of the Stanislavian people. There were those who said that, one day, he might be a candidate for President of Stanislavia.

That is why Colonel Zinfandel hated him.

Throughout his career, Gabriel Raffifi had been posted all around the world. For his first job, he worked in the Stanislavian Embassy in Austria. Then he went to Uruguay, where he helped to foil the notorious Pelotti gang. After that, promotions followed quickly, and he was appointed the Stanislavian ambassador to Latvia, then Canada, then Spain. Two years ago, he was posted to London and appointed the ambassador to Britain for the Democratic Republic of Stanislavia.

He lived in the Stanislavian Embassy in Kensington with his tall, beautiful wife, Maria, and their two children, Max and Natascha.

Max Raffifi was fifteen years old. He loved sport. A talented footballer, he played in midfield for his school team, and often wore the captain's armband. He was also one of the world's best young tennis players. In the holidays, the whole family often traveled to Maine, Buenos Aires or Auckland to watch Max playing in a tennis competition. He had won gold medals in the New Zealand Under-Sixteen Lawn Tennis Cup and the Argentinian Teenage Tennis Open finals. But he had never played at Wimbledon; that was his greatest ambition.

Natascha Raffifi was the baby of the family. She was twelve years old. She wasn't especially clever, beautiful or talented, but she always seemed to have a smile for everyone. Wherever she went, people remembered her fondly.

There is one more thing about Natascha Raffifi which is very important for this story. She owned a dog.

His name was Grk.

Because Gabriel Raffifi was a clever and experienced man, he immediately understood the true meaning behind the arrest of the President. He realized that Colonel Zinfandel had taken over Stanislavia, using the army and air force to impose his power on the population. At that very moment, his enemies would be fleeing for their lives.

That is why Gabriel Raffifi knew that he and his family must leave their house as quickly as possible. He told his wife that there was no time to pack. They would have to leave all their possessions behind.

His wife was shocked. "What about clothes?"

"We can buy some more."

"Can't we even take some money? And our passports?"

"There's no time," insisted Gabriel Raffifi. "We have to leave this minute."

"What about my tennis trophies?" asked Max.

"Your life is more important than your trophies," replied his father.

Natascha knew that there was no need to ask, "What about Grk?" Wherever they went, Grk was coming too. His life was just as important as theirs.

The whole family assembled in the hallway. Gabriel Raffifi said, "We're going to walk out of the house as if nothing is wrong. We will look calm and happy. We will have happy smiles our faces. That way, if any of Colonel Zinfandel's agents are watching us, it won't occur to them that we're running away. We will walk down the street to the car, get in and drive away. Everyone understand?"

They all nodded.

"Then let's go," said Gabriel Raffifi.

At that moment, the doorbell rang.

The whole family stood absolutely still. Even Grk didn't move a muscle. They stared at the door. Of course, they had no idea who was ringing the doorbell. Perhaps the postman was delivering a parcel. Perhaps the ambassador who lived next door had come to borrow a cup of sugar.

Gabriel Raffifi whispered: "Don't move. Keep quiet." He tiptoed to the front door, and peered through the spy-hole.

On the other side of the door, he could see five men in black suits and dark sunglasses. He recognized one of them: a lean, bony man, who had so little fat on his body that he looked like a walking skeleton. This was Major Raki, the chief of the Stanislavian Secret Service. Major Raki was renowned throughout Stanislavia for his cruelty. The mere mention of his name was often enough to make criminals confess to their crimes.

Gabriel Raffifi hurried back down the hallway, told his family to follow him and ran through the house to the kitchen. There was an exit at the bottom of the garden; from there, they could flee through Kensington, and get on the Underground.

When they reached the kitchen, they glanced through the French windows into the garden. On the other side of the glass, they could see five more men from the Stanislavian Secret Service standing on the lawn, waiting for them. There was no escape.

At that moment, they heard a terrible CRASH! It came from upstairs. The first crash was followed by another, and the sound of tearing wood.

Natascha was terrified. "What was that?"

"The front door," replied Max. "They've smashed it down."

"We can't escape," said their father. He knelt down, and wrapped his arms around his wife and two children. Grk cuddled up against them, and lifted his little pink tongue to lick Gabriel Raffifi's fingers. "Be brave," Gabriel whispered. "We have to be brave. Now, this is what we're going to do . . ."

When Major Raki, the chief of the Stanislavian Secret Service, walked into the kitchen, accompanied by two of his agents, they found the Raffifi family sitting at the table, playing a game of Snap as if they didn't have a care in the world. Grk was lying on the floor at Natascha's feet.

"Good morning," said Major Raki. When you saw him close up, he looked even more frightening. On his face, you could see the lines of his protruding cheekbones; on his fingers, you could see the bump of every knuckle and joint. Scrawled across his upper lip, he had a thin mustache which looked as if it had been drawn with a black crayon. He always wore dark glasses, even at night. It was said that no one, not even his mother, was permitted to see his eyes.

When Grk saw Major Raki, he started to growl.

"Good morning," replied Gabriel Raffifi. "Can we help you?"

"You certainly can," said Major Raki, and he stepped forward.

The bristles stood up on the back of Grk's neck, and he growled a little louder.

Major Raki said, "Gabriel Raffifi, by the order of Colonel Zinfandel, I put you and your family under arrest." Major Raki produced a pair of handcuffs from his pocket, and snapped them around Gabriel's wrists.

At that moment, Grk leaped forward. His jaws were wide open. But, before he could fly across the room and sink his white, sharp teeth into Major Raki's arm, Natascha grabbed him by the collar, and pulled him back. She didn't know what would happen to Grk if he managed to bite a chunk out of Major Raki's bony forearm, but she guessed that it wouldn't be anything nice.

"This way, please," said Major Raki. "All of you. Follow me."

Max said, "Where are we going?"

"No talking!" snapped Major Raki. "Follow me."

Major Raki walked out of the kitchen, and up the stairs. The Raffifi family followed him. They had no choice, and no chance to escape: ten guards from the Stanislavian Secret Service watched every move that they made.

In the street, a white van had been parked outside the house. One of the guards unlocked the back doors, and ordered the family to climb inside.

The family got into the van. As the guard prepared to slam the doors, locking the family inside, Major Raki shouted, "Stop!" All the guards looked at him. "The dog," ordered Major Raki. "Get rid of the dog."

"No," whispered Natascha. "No, please." She wrapped her arms around Grk, and held him to her chest.

Three guards climbed into the back of the van. Natascha struggled desperately, but the guards were stronger than her. One of them held her arms, and another grabbed Grk.

Why didn't the rest of her family help? Because they would have been killed. Inside the van, where no passersby could see what was happening, the third guard had pulled a pistol from his jacket. He pointed the pistol at Max, Maria and Gabriel Raffifi. "Anybody moves, I shoot. Understand?"

So no one moved.

Except Grk.

Grk turned his head, and opened his jaws, and sank his sharp, white teeth into the fleshy palm of the guard who was holding him. The guard screamed, dropped Grk and stared at his hand. Blood spurted from several neat little tooth-shaped wounds.

Grk landed on the floor of the van. He whirled around and sank his teeth into the second guard's ankle. Unfortunately, the second guard was wearing thick leather boots, and Grk's teeth were very small. He couldn't bite through the leather. The guard, a fat, brutal man, lifted his boot, and delivered a short, hard kick in the middle of Grk's stomach.

Grk squealed, and rolled over. His paws scrabbled to get a grip on the floor, but he wasn't quick enough. The guard kicked him again, harder.

Grk shot out of the van, spun through the air and landed in the road. He lay on the tarmac, not moving.

Natascha leaped up and tried to jump out after him, but her mother pulled her back. She knew what would happen if they disobeyed the guards.

The guards got out of the van, slammed the door, locked it and signaled to the driver that he could go. The driver started the engine.

If anyone had been walking along Rudolph Gardens, they would have seen a strange sight: a white van, accelerating down the road, and, peering through the back window, two desperate little faces.

Max stared at their house, wondering whether he would ever see it again.

Natascha had eyes only for one thing. She watched Grk, who was lying in the road, curled up, not moving. Natascha stared at Grk until the van turned the corner at the end of the road, and she could no longer see him.

12

When the van had gone, Grk lifted himself onto his feet and staggered to the side of the road. He didn't want to be run over by a passing car. He lay on the pavement and licked his wounds.

He lay there for several hours, hoping that Natascha would come back. He didn't understand where she had gone, or why.

By nightfall, Grk had started to feel an unpleasant sensation in his stomach.

Emptiness. A terrible emptiness.

Hour by hour, his stomach felt emptier and emptier.

Until Grk had no choice. He had to find some food. He trotted along the pavement, leaving the house behind him, and searched for food. He found a piece of bread in a dustbin, and ate that. Later, he found a half-eaten kebab in the road, and ate that too.

When his stomach was a little less empty, Grk tried to find his way back to Rudolph Gardens, but couldn't. He was lost.

For several days, Grk wandered round London, lost, lonely and frightened. He scavenged food. He dodged cars and lorries. He slept in parks, or curled under a pile of cardboard boxes. He was kicked, and chased, and almost run over.

Then he found Tim.

13

If you are easily shocked, please skip this chapter, and proceed directly to Chapter 14.

You should only read the following pages if you can read descriptions of the most horrible events without shaking, shivering or shutting your eyes. I hope you never have to experience events such as these.

This is your last chance. If you want to avoid descriptions of horrible events, go straight to Chapter 14.

Anyone left?

Good. Then, let's continue.

You will remember that the Raffifi family were marched out of their house in Rudolph Gardens and thrust into a white van, where they were guarded by several men from the Stanislavian Secret Service.

The van drove for two hours. Gabriel Raffifi told the children to keep calm, and not worry about the future. He promised them that everything was going to be okay. All of them were scared, but they were brave, so they didn't show what they were feeling. They pretended that everything was normal. They talked in low, quiet voices, and discussed normal things: what they would like for lunch, and the weather forecast, and where Max might play his next game of tennis. Of them all, Natascha was the most frightened, and she could barely bring herself to speak. She couldn't stop thinking about Grk, and wondering what had happened to him. Natascha was the youngest member of the family, so no one would have been surprised if she had cried or started trembling. But she was exceptionally brave. She sat in the corner of the van, kept a smile on her face and tried to take part in the conversation.

After two hours, the van stopped, and the back doors were opened. The Raffifis clambered out, and found themselves standing on a large, wide, empty expanse of tarmac. Some flags were fluttering in the breeze. A few squat buildings overlooked them. A small jet airplane waited nearby. Just as Gabriel Raffifi had suspected, they were going to be flown back to Stanislavia.

If there had been any way to escape, Gabriel Raffifi would have taken it. He knew that Colonel Zinfandel was waiting in Stanislavia–and there wasn't a man on the planet whom Gabriel Raffifi feared and hated more than Colonel Zinfandel. However, escape was impossible. When the guards ordered them to get into the airplane, Mr. Raffifi nodded to his family. They did as they were asked.

The small plane had ten seats. The Raffifi family occupied four, and six were taken by men from the Stanislavian Secret Service, including a lean man dressed in a black suit and black sunglasses. Major Raki smiled and nodded at the Raffifi family, who pretended that they hadn't seen him. They took their seats on the plane as if they were flying away on holiday. Max and Natascha even argued about which of them should sit by the window. Natascha won. As the youngest, she was always allowed to win those kinds of arguments.

When everyone was strapped into their seats, the plane taxied along the runway and took off.

As I said, I want to make this chapter as short and painless as possible. The events described here are unpleasant. Let's hope that such things never happen to us or anyone we love.

The flight to Vilnetto took about three hours. The plane landed at a small airport outside the city. A convoy of military trucks was waiting, accompanied by a group of fifty soldiers from the Stanislavian Army.

When Mr. Raffifi saw all these soldiers, he laughed. "Who do they think we are? Do they really need fifty soldiers to stop us escaping? A peace-loving man, and his wife and their two children. What could we possibly do against fifty soldiers?"

His wife and children smiled, pretending that they too were amused and they too were feeling brave, but it was pretty difficult to carry on with this pretense. Things weren't looking good. None of them said a word. They knew that they wouldn't be able to speak without sounding frightened. In those circumstances, it's best to keep silent.

Major Raki walked past the Raffifi family, snapped his heels and stood to attention. The sun reflected off his dark glasses. He muttered a few words to the soldiers. Ten men surrounded the Raffifi family. Five of the soldiers stood beside Mr. and Mrs. Raffifi. The other five soldiers stood beside Max and Natascha.

Major Raki smiled. "Mrs. Raffifi, you may say goodbye to your children. And you, Mr. Raffifi, the same."

Mr. and Mrs. Raffifi glanced at one another. Then, they both nodded. They knew that nothing could be gained by protesting or arguing. Mrs. Raffifi hugged each of her children in turn. Her husband did too. Then, they allowed themselves to be led away by the soldiers, who shoved them into the back of a green military truck. Just before she got into the truck, Mrs. Raffifi turned and waved. Max and Natascha waved back. Then, one of the soldiers raised his heavy hand, and pushed Mrs. Raffifi into the truck.

Tears were streaming down Natascha's face. Max managed not to cry; he knew it was important to remain proud and dignified in front of such horrible people.

Neither of them would have admitted it, but both Max and Natascha thought that they would never see their parents again.

It pains me to tell you this, but they were right.

• • •

The two children were forced to clamber into the back of another green military truck. Inside, Max and Natascha squatted on the floor. Soldiers surrounded them. With a judder, the truck's engine started, and they drove away.

The back of the truck had no windows, so they couldn't see where they were going. They heard noises: the chatter of birds, the shouts of people selling newspapers, the roar of traffic. After they had been driving for ten or fifteen minutes, Max turned to his sister and said, "At least we're home in Stanislavia."

"That's right," said Natascha, pretending to be much braver than she actually felt. "It's always good to be home."

Max looked at the soldier who was sitting next to them. He was an ugly brute whose fat face was covered with red spots. Max said, "Where are you taking us?"

"No talking," snarled the soldier.

"I want to know where you're taking us."

"No talking!" The soldier raised his fist, threatening to hit Max.

Max slumped back onto the floor, and kept quiet.

After fifteen or twenty minutes, the truck stopped. From outside, there was the sound of conversation. The truck moved again, drove for another minute, then stopped. Bang! Bang! Someone rapped against the side of the truck. "Out," snarled the ugly soldier. "Get out. Go on! Go on!"

Max and Natascha did as he asked. They scrambled down to the end of the truck, and clambered out.

They found themselves in a narrow courtyard. High, windowless walls rose on all four sides. Several soldiers watched them. Every soldier carried a Kalashnikov. (In case you don't know, a Kalashnikov is a type of machine gun.)

Max turned to the ugly soldier who had accompanied them in the lorry, and asked, "Where are we?"

"If you say one more word, I shall shoot you," replied the soldier. "Understand?"

Max nodded. He was tempted to say yes, but he didn't want to give the soldier any excuse for shooting him.

"Good," said the ugly soldier. "Now, both of you, follow me."

He led Max and Natascha across the courtyard to a narrow doorway. They climbed a flight of stone steps, and walked down a long, cold corridor, past a line of closed doors. Finally, they reached an open door. A man was waiting beside it. A bunch of forty keys hung from his belt. He nodded to the ugly soldier, who pushed the children into the room, and slammed the door after them.

Max and Natascha looked around the room. It was roughly the same size as each of their bedrooms in the house in Rudolph Gardens. However, this cell didn't have carpets, books, pictures on the walls or any of the things that had made their bedrooms so cozy and comfortable. Instead, the cell had two metal beds, two metal buckets, gray floors, gray walls and not much else. There wasn't even a window. The only light came from a single bare bulb hanging from the center of the ceiling.

Natascha pointed at the two buckets. "What are those for?"

Max looked at her. "Um. Well. It's . . ."

Before he said another word, Natascha worked it out for herself. She grinned. "Then, there's one good thing about this place."

"Oh, yes? What's that?"

"We both get our own toilet."

What she said wasn't specially funny, but Max couldn't help laughing. His laughter was infectious. It seemed like the first time that either of them had laughed for days and days. And it felt good. The two of them laughed as if they had just heard the funniest joke in the world. They clutched their bellies. Their faces went pink, and tears rolled down their cheeks.

At the other end of the corridor, three of the prison guards were playing poker. They heard the sound of laughter coming from one of the cells. The guards were bemused. One of them said, "It's those kids. The Raffifi kids. You know? The two kids who got picked up in London."

"Maybe they're going a bit mad," said another of the guards.

The third guard said, "I would be, if I was them."

The three guards sat in silence for a minute, wondering how they would feel if they were the Raffifi children–taken from their home, separated from their parents, locked in a prison cell. Then, one of guards said, "Whose deal is it?"

"Mine," said another, and he started dealing the cards.

Max and Natascha discovered that prison life has a simple routine. At six o'clock in the morning, a guard delivered breakfast, which consisted of bread and water. At midday, another guard delivered bread, water and some tasteless soup for lunch. At six o'clock in the evening, supper arrived: water, bread and a hunk of rubbery yellow cheese. In the afternoon, the children were escorted to the yard, where they walked around in the fresh air for an hour. In the evening, they were led to the latrines, where they emptied their buckets down the drain. And that was it. There was nothing to do. No books, no music, no telly, nothing. The Raffifi children were strong-minded and intelligent, but they quickly slumped into boredom and depression.

One night, their routine was broken: they had a visitor.

Supper had been delivered and eaten. The two children were lying on their beds. They had run out of things to say, but they tried to keep talking, just to avoid the terrible silence. One of the best ways to banish silence, they had discovered, is playing a game. They had tried I Spy, but there wasn't much to see in their cramped, gray prison cell. After wall, bed and bucket, they ran out of things to spy. So they played Twenty Questions.

Max said, "Are you male?"

"Yes."

"Are you real?"

"Yes."

"Are you still alive?"

"Yes. That's three questions."

Max thought for a minute. "Do you work with animals?"

"Yes." Natascha giggled. "That's a good guess. How did you know?"

"Because I know you. Okay, let me think. Do you–"

But Max didn't get a chance to ask his next question, because the door swung open, and two tall soldiers hurried into the room. "Get up," snapped the first soldier. "On your feet!"

Neither of the children moved. They didn't like being

told what to do. Max looked at the soldiers and said, "Why should we?"

"If you don't, I'll hit you," said one of the soldiers, and he made his fist into a ball.

Not wanting to be hit, Max and Natascha rolled off their bunks, and staggered to their feet.

Two more soldiers hurried into the room and took up positions by the door. Each of them was wearing the uniform of the Imperial Guard, the elite troops of the Stanislavian Army: black boots, green trousers, a green jacket and a black beret. They were carrying Kalashnikovs.

A man walked into the room, and the four soldiers snapped to attention, clicking their heels, and straightening their backs. The man ignored them. He looked at the children. "So, you are the Raffifis. Am I right?"

Neither of the children replied.

The man continued as if he didn't care. He pointed at each of them in turn. "You must be Max, and you must be Natascha. How nice to meet you. I hope you're comfortable in your new home."

Of course, he was being sarcastic. He knew that the children couldn't possibly be comfortable, because the cell was cramped, dark and smelly. But he was the type of man who enjoyed behaving like a sarcastic bully, particularly to small children who couldn't possibly fight back.

Who was this vile and horrible man? He was the notorious Colonel Zinfandel.

Colonel Zinfandel was a short, well-built man, with a muscular body. He had black hair, a straight nose and lean cheekbones. He was clean-shaven, and handsome. Most women found him very attractive, and a lot of men too.

That was one of the secrets of his success. He had used his good looks to get power for himself.

He had started life in a small village, somewhere in the mountains of Stanislavia. His father was a shepherd with twenty goats, and his mother made cheese from the goats' milk. Now, fifty-five years later, his parents were dead, but Colonel Zinfandel was the President of Stanislavia.

Colonel Zinfandel only wore military uniform on special occasions. Ordinarily, he wore an expensive black woolen suit, a white silk shirt, a blue silk tie and shiny black leather shoes. Every day, one of his servants polished his shoes for an hour, until you could see your face in them.

Max and Natascha stared at Colonel Zinfandel. They were very frightened, but they were determined not to show any fear. If you show your enemy that you're frightened, you make him even stronger. Each of the Raffifi children made a great effort to keep a calm expression on their faces, and show no fear. Natascha found this very difficult. Max was better at hiding his feelings. He was older, so he had had more practice.

Colonel Zinfandel pointed at the tray. "How is the food? You like it?"

Neither of them answered.

Colonel Zinfandel chuckled. "It must be nice to have some real Stanislavian food, rather than that English rubbish."

Max cleared his throat, because he didn't want his voice to sound reedy or frail. Then he said, "Since we were locked in this place, we have eaten nothing except watery soup and tasteless stew and stale bread. That isn't real Stanislavian food."

Colonel Zinfandel stared at Max. He wasn't used to people answering back. "Oh? And what would you prefer?"

"Real Stanislavian food is beef goulash and dumplings and poppy-seed pastries. Not the muck that you serve in here."

When the soldiers heard Max, they couldn't help being impressed. No one dared to speak to Colonel Zinfandel like that. But none of them showed their true feelings. They didn't want to be sent to work in the salt mines for the next twenty years.

"And another thing," said Max. "English food isn't as bad as people say. You obviously haven't been to England, have you?"

"You're a brave boy," said Colonel Zinfandel, not answering Max's question. "Not many people would dare to speak to me like that. Most people would have a little more respect."

Max shrugged his shoulders. "Why should I have any respect for someone like you?"

"I'll tell you one reason," said Colonel Zinfandel. "If I snapped my fingers, one of these soldiers would take his gun and shoot you dead."

"You wouldn't dare do anything like that," said Max.

Colonel Zinfandel smiled. "Don't test my patience, little boy. You might get a nasty surprise."

"I don't think so," said Max. "What could be nastier than being here and seeing you?"

Colonel Zinfandel didn't reply. It was one of the few moments in that vile man's life when he was completely speechless. But his face went bright red. His eyes darkened. He clenched his teeth.

Everyone knew that when Colonel Zinfandel got angry, he was dangerous. Anyone sensible would have taken this opportunity to apologize or hide. Not Max. He stood even straighter, and spoke even louder. "You must let us out of here. You have no right to hold us in prison."

The color of Colonel Zinfandel's face turned an even deeper shade of red. No one dared talk to him like this! No one! But he didn't want his soldiers to know that this little boy had made him angry. So he laughed. His laughter sounded twisted and strange. He stopped laughing and hissed: "Little boy, do you want to know how long you and your sister will be confined in this prison?"

"Yes, please," said Max. "I'd like that very much."

"For the rest of your lives," whispered Colonel Zinfandel. With those words, he turned around and stalked out of the cell. The soldiers followed him. The last soldier slammed the heavy door, and turned the key in the lock. The sound of the turning key seemed to reverberate for a long time.

Natascha Raffifi lifted her head and looked at her elder brother. Her voice was quiet and frightened. "Are we really going to be here for the rest of our lives?"

"Of course not," said Max. "Don't be silly, Natascha."

"How do you know?"

"Because I do. We'll be out of here within a few days. There's no way that we'll be staying here for more than a week."

But Max didn't believe the words that he had just spoken. In his heart, he thought the two of them would be staying in this prison until the day that they died. That was what Natascha thought too. They lay down on their separate beds. Although they tried to hide their true feelings from the other, each of them felt a deep sense of despair.

A tear trickled down Natascha's cheek. She wiped it away before Max noticed, and turned her head to face the wall.

14

Thirty thousand feet above the surface of the earth, Tim and Grk were eating smoked salmon sandwiches.

The sandwiches were served on a china plate. While Tim and Grk were eating, the stewardess brought regular refills for their drinks: orange juice in a glass for Tim, fresh spring water in a bowl for Grk. She also brought thick linen napkins and little bags of cashew nuts. From now on, Tim decided, he never wanted to fly anything except First Class.

The flight took about three hours. There wasn't a movie, but the stewardess brought a book that another passenger had left behind on a previous flight. Tim read the first few pages, then skimmed through the pictures in the in-flight magazine. Mostly, he stared out of the window and watched the clouds passing under the airplane. From where Tim was sitting, the clouds looked like mountains and valleys. If you didn't know better, you might think that you were flying over a country where every field, house and tree had been covered with a layer of thick white snow.

When the plane landed in Vilnetto, Tim and Grk were the first people to leave. That's what happens when you're a VIP. The stewards and the stewardesses queued up to say goodbye. Even the captain came out of his cockpit to shake Tim's hand, and pat Grk on the head.

Tim and Grk walked out of the plane, and into the blinding sunshine. The air was warm. A line of steps stretched down to the tarmac, where two men were waiting. One of them was dressed in a green uniform with shiny silver buttons. The other was dressed in a blue uniform with shiny silver buttons.

As Tim and Grk walked down the steps, the two men saluted. "Good morning," said the man in the green uniform. "Welcome to Stanislavia."

"Thanks," said Tim.

"At your service," said the man in the blue uniform. He stuck out his hand. Tim shook hands with him. Then Tim shook hands with the first man. Then the two men shook hands with one another. When they had finished, the man in the blue uniform nodded to Tim. "Come this way, please."

The two men started walking towards the airport, and Tim hurried behind them. He didn't know what was going on, but he thought it was best not to argue.

The two men glanced at Tim, and Grk, and the piece of string tied to Grk's collar. They were impressed. Their job involved escorting VIPs through the airport, and they knew that only the richest and most important people would use a piece of string as a dog's lead. A Quite Important Person would have used an expensive leather lead with silver buckles. Only Very Important People don't have to show off and prove how important they are, because everyone already knows how important they are.

The four of them reached Passports and Customs. A policeman glanced at Tim's passport, then waved him on. Everyone in the airport had already been warned to expect the arrival of a VIP. They hurried through Customs, and into the car park, where a large black Mercedes was waiting. A man in a black uniform and a peaked cap was holding one of the doors open. He was the driver. "Good morning," he said. "Welcome to Stanislavia."

"Thanks," said Tim.

"I am your driver for today." The driver smiled. "How do you like our beautiful country?"

"It's okay," said Tim.

"Only okay?"

"Yes."

"Is not beautiful? Is not wonderful?"

"I've only just arrived," said Tim. "So I don't really know what it's like. But it seems okay."

The three men looked a bit disappointed. They had wanted Tim to say that their country was the most beautiful place that he had ever seen. But they were too polite to argue, so they took turns to shake hands with Tim, then shook hands with one another, then shook hands with Tim again. When they had finished, the man in the blue uniform said, "Where is your destination, please? The driver will take you there immediately."

"I'm looking for someone," said Tim.

"Oh, yes? And for whom are you looking?"

"Her name is Natascha."

"Natascha? Oh, it is beautiful name!"

The man in the green uniform nodded. "A beautiful Stanislavian name!"

The man in the black uniform asked, "Where does she live, this Natascha?"

"I don't know."

"We will find her," said the man in the green uniform. "What is her second name? She is called Natascha What?"

"I don't know," said Tim.

"You don't know?"

"No." Tim shook his head. "I just know she's called Natascha."

"This is difficult," said the man in the blue uniform. "In our country, we have many women."

The man in the green uniform nodded. "And many of them are called Natascha."

The man in the black uniform said, "What does she look like? This Natascha? She is beautiful, of course, because she is Stanislavian woman, and all Stanislavian women are beautiful. But how does she look? Black hair? Brown hair? Blond hair? How?"

"I don't know," said Tim. "I've never met her."

The three men looked at one another. Now, they were puzzled. And not just puzzled. They were also a little bit worried. The first to speak was the man in the green uniform. "Do you know anything about this woman? This Natascha?"

"Yes," said Tim. "She's the owner of this dog." He pointed at Grk.

The three men stared at Grk, as if he might be able to help them. Grk wagged his tail.

"This is not big help," said the man in the blue uniform.

"But he is nice dog," said the man in the green uniform.

"Very nice dog," said the man in the black uniform. "What is his name? Or perhaps you do not know that either?"

"His name is Grk," said Tim.

The three men nodded. They told Tim that Grk was an excellent name for a dog. Each of them took turns to lean down and tickle Grk behind his ears. Then they stood up, and looked at Tim. The man in the green uniform said, "You know nothing else about this Natascha or this Grk?"

"Actually, I do," said Tim. "One other thing."

The three men leaned forward.

Tim said, "Natascha lived in London."

The three men nodded.

Tim continued. "Her father was the ambassador. Your country's ambassador to Britain."

For a second, there was total silence. Then the three men spoke at once.

The man in the green uniform said, "The Ambassador!"

The man in the blue uniform said, "Natascha Raffifi!"

The man in the black uniform said, "Raffifi! Raffifi! Raffifi!"

Tim looked at them. He didn't have a clue what was

going on. The three men started chattering excitedly in their own language. Tim couldn't understand what they were saying, because he couldn't speak a single word of Stanislavian. (Actually, that's not quite true. He could speak one word. He could say "Grk." But he didn't know that "Grk" was a word in the Stanislavian language, so it doesn't really count.)

After a couple of minutes, the three men asked Tim and Grk to get inside the Mercedes. They closed the door. Then, the driver sat in the front, and the other two men ran back to the airport, where they made several frantic phone calls.

15

About twenty minutes later, the two men returned. They whispered to the driver, who turned slightly pale.

The two men opened the back door, and looked at Tim. This time, they didn't shake hands with him.

The man in the green uniform said, "We have discovered the whereabouts of Natascha Raffifi."

The man in the blue uniform nodded, but didn't speak.

Tim felt a bit nervous. The two men were behaving strangely. He said, "Where is she?"

The man in the green uniform said, "Enjoy your stay in Stanislavia."

"Goodbye," said the man in the blue uniform.

Tim was just about to ask why they hadn't answered his question, when one of the men slammed the door, locking Tim inside the car.

The driver started the engine, and the Mercedes rolled forwards along the road.

16

They drove in silence. In the front, the driver concentrated on the road. In the back, Tim stared out of the window, and Grk sprawled on the leather seat beside him, dozing. Every now and then, Grk yawned. His stomach was still digesting the smoked salmon sandwiches, so he had no energy to spare. For Grk, digestion was a serious business.

They drove along a motorway. Something seemed very peculiar. After a few minutes, Tim worked out what it was: they were driving on the wrong side of the road. There was no need to panic, because everyone else was doing it too.

The motorway was packed with interesting cars. Tim stared out of the window, and watched them go past. He had only been abroad a few times, holidaying with his mother and father, so he was very excited to be traveling through a foreign country. He noticed lots of things that were different from Britain: the number plates; the road signs; even the drivers looked different, and they never stopped hooting their horns.

In the distance, he saw a huge building, built of gray concrete. As they drove closer, he noticed that the building had few windows, and was surrounded by high walls. Rolls of barbed wire ran along the top of the walls. Armed guards were parading outside the front gates. Tim was relieved when they drove past the building; for a moment, he had been worried that he was being taken there. He leaned forwards, and spoke to the driver. "Excuse me. What was that building?"

"That? Is the State Prison. You understand? Prison?"

"Yes, yes," said Tim. "I understand."

There was a long pause. The driver seemed to be thinking. Finally, he said, "She is there. Your friend."

"Who? Natascha?"

"Yes. With her brother also."

Tim was extremely surprised. He couldn't imagine why a young girl, the same age as him, should be put in prison. "Why? What have they done?"

"Bad things."

"But, what?"

"Is better if you do not ask questions."

"I want to know," said Tim. "Please, tell me. What did they do?"

"Is not possible. No more questions."

"If you tell me, I won't ask anything else," pleaded Tim. "Why are they in prison?"

Rather than answering, the driver pressed a button on his dashboard. A glass panel slid across the middle of the car, dividing his section from Tim's section. Now, the driver couldn't even hear what Tim was saying.

Tim felt offended. The driver was very rude. Tim slumped back in the seat, then turned around, and stared at the prison. It was dwindling into the distance. He wondered what Natascha could have done to deserve being put in a gray, high-walled place like that.

You can understand why Tim was offended by the driver's rudeness. However, he shouldn't have been. He didn't understand what it was like to live in Stanislavia at that time. He didn't know that, since Colonel Zinfandel had taken over the country, you couldn't ask questions. You never knew who might be listening. You never knew who was a spy. You never knew who would report exactly what you said to the Secret Service. You never knew when Colonel Zinfandel's men would break down your front door, snap handcuffs around your wrists and drag you to prison.

Since the day that Colonel Zinfandel proclaimed himself president, Stanislavia was not a happy country.

17

While Tim and Grk were driving into the center of Vilnetto in a big black Mercedes, events had been moving fast in Britain and Stanislavia. Phone lines had been buzzing. A British Ambassador had been summoned from his breakfast; he wasn't pleased, because he had been breakfasting on crispy bacon, scrambled eggs and a cup of strong tea. A Chief of Police had been summoned from his elevenses of black coffee and an almond croissant. All this had happened because Mr. Malt found a note on his computer keyboard.

Dear Mum and Dad,

I have gone to Stanislavia to return Grk to his owners. I will be back when I have found them. Sorry about

taking the money, but I need it. Please debit my pocket money for the next 183 weeks.
Love from
Tim

When Mr. Malt found that note, he read it a couple of times, and laughed, thinking that Tim was playing a joke. He glanced at his watch, and looked at the date. No, it wasn't April 1. And Tim didn't make a habit of playing practical jokes. Mr. Malt scratched his head, and read the note for a third time. Then he carried it downstairs, and said to his wife, "What do you think of this?"

"Don't bother me now," said Mrs. Malt. "I'm trying to think."

"Maybe you should read this."

"I don't have time."

"It might be important."

Mrs. Malt shook her head. "I'm sure it is to you, dear, but I'm worried about Tim. And if you had a heart, you'd be worried too."

"I am worried," said Mr. Malt. "That's why I think you should read this." He thrust the note at his wife.

She took it, and glanced at the words written on the paper. She read them again. Her face went white. She staggered, and sat down at the table. Then she read the words for a third time. Her voice was a whisper: "Do you . . . Do you think it's true?"

"I think it must be," said Mr. Malt. "He's gone to Stanis . . . Stanism . . . Stanistic . . . You know, that place."

Mrs. Malt looked at the note, and read the word aloud. "Stanislavia."

"That's right," replied Mr. Malt. "That one. He's gone there."

"How can we stop him?"

They looked at one another. Without another word, Mr. Malt dashed for the phone, and dialed 999. When the operator answered, Mr. Malt asked to be connected directly to the police.

Mr. Malt spoke to a policeman who thought he was joking. However, the policeman took his details, then promised to make a few enquiries and ring back.

Five minutes later, the policeman rang back. This time, his voice sounded quite different. Now, he knew that Mr. Malt hadn't been joking. The policeman had spoken to some people who worked in Heathrow Airport. Using their computer, they had confirmed that a young boy called Timothy Malt, accompanied by a dog, had boarded a plane which flew from London to Stanislavia. It was too late to stop Tim leaving the country, because he had already left.

A couple of days ago, Mr. Malt had hardly heard of Stanislavia. Now, his only child had flown there. What was the world coming to? Trying to keep his voice calm, he asked the policeman a simple question. "How are you going to find my son?"

"Don't worry, sir," said the policeman. "Everything's going to be fine."

"Don't worry? Don't worry? How could I not worry? My son has disappeared! And he's gone to a country that I can't even pronounce!"

"I understand your concern," said the policeman. "But we're doing everything in our power to locate him."

And they were. The Metropolitan Police had immediately contacted all the relevant people who would be able to find Tim: Interpol, the Foreign Office, the Stanislavian Ambassador in London and the British Ambassador in Vilnetto. Phone calls, e-mails and faxes were bouncing across the surface of Europe, and lots of breakfasts were being interrupted. Cups of coffee were growing cold. Croissants were left half-eaten.

"Just tell me this," said Mr. Malt. "Do you know where he is?"

The policeman said, "I appreciate how difficult this must be, sir, but I have to ask you to be patient."

"Patient?" shouted Mr. Malt. "Patient? When are you going to find my son?"

"As soon as we can."

Mr. Malt would have liked to carry on shouting, but he realized that there wasn't much point. So he put down the phone. He sat at the kitchen table opposite his wife. They looked at one another.

After a minute or two, Mrs. Malt said, "Terence?"

"Yes?"

"Do you think it's our fault?"

"No," said Mr. Malt. "Of course not."

But he didn't sound as if he believed it.

Several hundred miles away, in the pocket of a black suit, a telephone rang. The suit belonged to Major Raki. He put his hand into his pocket, removed the phone and lifted it to his ear. He listened for a few minutes, asked two questions, then ended the call. He put his phone back in his pocket, and went to find his boss.

That morning, like most mornings, Colonel Zinfandel was boxing.

Wherever he went, Colonel Zinfandel took his boxing gloves, his boxing shorts, his boxing shoes and a couple of soldiers from the army who were skillful boxers. The soldiers were twenty years younger than Colonel Zinfandel, but he was a match for them. Their youth gave them strength and fitness, but Colonel Zinfandel had more cunning. Most mornings, he won.

There was only one rule in the match: the soldiers weren't allowed to hit Colonel Zinfandel's face. Colonel Zinfandel was exceedingly proud of his long, slim nose, and he would have been furious if a soldier's fist had broken it.

In a state room of the Imperial Palace, Colonel Zinfandel's carpenters had built a boxing ring. It had ropes round the sides and a cushioned floor to protect anyone who fell over–or got knocked over. Every morning, Colonel Zinfandel and a young soldier pranced around the ring, trading blows.

Usually, the match would continue until one of the men was knocked to the ground. Today, however, the match was interrupted by the arrival of Major Raki, who stood by the side of the ring and raised his hand, signaling that he had something important to say.

Inside the ring, the two men dropped their hands to their sides. Both of them were sweating and breathing heavily. Colonel Zinfandel always got very angry when his boxing match was interrupted. He looked at Major Raki, and hissed, "I hope you have a very good reason for stopping this match."

Major Raki quickly explained what he had been told by the telephone call.

When Major Raki had finished, Colonel Zinfandel pressed his boxing gloves together. If he hadn't been wearing gloves, he would have rubbed his hands. "I would like to meet this boy. What is his name?"

"Timothy Malt."

"Yes, this Timothy Malt. Bring him to me."

"Now?"

"Yes," said Colonel Zinfandel. "Now."

"Yes, sir." Major Raki hurried away.

Colonel Zinfandel lifted his gloves, and turned to look at the young soldier who had been boxing with him. "Where were we?"

Before the soldier had time to answer, Colonel Zinfandel flung out his fist and punched the soldier's face. The soldier sprawled across the boxing ring, clattered to the floor and lay there groaning. Blood dribbled from his nose. Colonel Zinfandel grinned. Today was going to be a good day. He could feel it in his bones.

18

Vilnetto is a small city. To the north, you can see the high mountains which protect Stanislavia from its nearest neighbors. To the south, a fertile plain stretches for many miles. In the summer, the city is so hot that you can hardly breathe; during the winter, snow covers the roofs and the pavements. In many ways, this is a difficult place for people to live, and the difficulties have been made even worse by the complicated political situation in the country. In the past fifty years, however, Stanislavia embraced democracy, and the country grew happier. The inhabitants were richer and more comfortable. When you have glass in your windows, tiles on your roof and food in your belly, the weather doesn't matter so much.

Beautiful old streets sneak through the center of the city. The houses are tall, slim and well proportioned. Fountains cascade day and night. The cobbled streets are narrow, so large lorries cannot venture down them. Even driving a car is slow and difficult. Most people travel on foot or by bicycle. Therefore, the air is quiet, and not polluted by stinking fumes.

On the eastern side of the city, near the banks of the river, the Royal Family of Stanislavia built their palace. The first foundations were laid in 1541. Over the following centuries, the Imperial Palace grew larger and more ornate. Kings and Queens of Stanislavia built themselves a huge complex of ballrooms, bedrooms and stables. It shouldn't have been any surprise to them when the Stanislavian population rose up in fury, overthrew the monarchy and put a democratically elected government in its place.

(Incidentally, the current King and Queen of Stanislavia live in New York. The King is a computer salesman and the Queen breeds dachshunds. Neither of them speaks a single word of Stanislavian, and they have no plans to visit the country. Only two or three of their closest friends even know that they're a King and a Queen. All their other friends and neighbors just know them as Mr. and Mrs. Castle, that nice couple who never go anywhere without those funny little sausage dogs.)

The front entrance of the Imperial Palace is used for ceremonial occasions. A few soldiers stand beside the golden gates, wearing fancy uniforms. If you're a tourist, you might ask a passerby to take your photo standing beside one of the soldiers.

However, if you are visiting the Palace for business, you

will probably enter by the other entrance, round the back. That entrance has a single black gate. Ten soldiers watch every car that enters or leaves.

Colonel Zinfandel knew that the population of the country didn't like him. He knew that the people would prefer to have their own elected President back again. So, he surrounded the Palace with hundreds of soldiers. Colonel Zinfandel was taking no chances.

A black Mercedes stopped beside the back entrance to the Palace. The driver wound down his window, and handed his identity card to the guards.

One of the guards examined the driver's identity card, checking that the driver really did look like his photo. Another guard peered through the back window, and took a long look at the passengers. The guard saw a boy and a dog. Both of them looked harmless.

The guards waved the car forwards. The driver accelerated. The Mercedes pulled through the black gate, and drove into the Palace.

The Mercedes passed high walls, and windows covered with thick metal bars, and twenty soldiers marching in rhythm. Through the window, Tim saw several tanks, a lorry, two jeeps and a helicopter, all painted in military green. Then the car stopped. The driver got out, and walked round to Tim's door. "Please," said the driver. "You will get out now."

Tim got out of the car, and stood on the tarmac, holding the piece of string that was still tied around Grk's collar.

Tim noticed that three men were walking towards him.

Two of them were wearing green military uniforms. The third, who walked ahead of the other two, was wearing a black suit, a white shirt, a black tie and a pair of black sunglasses.

Tim noticed something else. The hair around Grk's neck was standing upright.

Tim didn't know very much about dogs, so he didn't understand what that meant. He didn't know that when dogs are angry, the hair on their neck stands up.

The three men stopped beside Tim. The man in the black sunglasses said, "Good morning. You are Timothy Malt?"

"Yes," said Tim.

"Very good," said Major Raki–who was, of course, the man in the black sunglasses. "You will come with me."

"Where are we going?"

Major Raki didn't answer. He turned on his heel, and waited for Tim to follow.

If Tim had been braver or more foolish, he would have argued. But he was both scared and intelligent. So he followed Major Raki.

Grk was brave and foolish. But he was tied to Tim's hand by a piece of string. So he followed too.

The five of them marched across the courtyard in a neat formation: one of the soldiers walked first, followed by Major Raki, Tim and Grk in a line, and the second soldier followed at the back. No one spoke.

They crossed the courtyard, ducked under a low doorway, turned a corner and walked down a long corridor. Men and women were hurrying from doorway to doorway.

When they noticed Major Raki, all of them did exactly the same thing: they stopped whatever they were doing, snapped their heels together and saluted. Major Raki saluted back.

Lots of questions were rushing around Tim's mind. Questions like "What am I doing here?" and "Who are all these people?" and "Why does this man never take off his sunglasses?" However, Tim felt so rushed and confused that he didn't try to answer any of the questions. He just hurried to keep up with the Major and the two soldiers.

Every few paces, Grk glanced at Major Raki, and sniffed the air. Yes, he recognized that smell. He knew its owner. That was the man who had come to 23 Rudolph Gardens, taken the Raffifi family and forced them to climb into the back of a white van. Grk growled–but he growled so quietly that no one could hear him.

It's always difficult to know what a dog is thinking, but I can guess what Grk was thinking at that moment. He was thinking, I can't bite this man now, but I'll do it soon. And when I do, I'll give him a bite that he'll never forget.

At the end of the corridor, they reached a pair of wooden doors. Two soldiers stood by these doors, one on either side. The soldiers were wearing black berets and holding Kalashnikovs slung around their shoulders on black leather straps. Both soldiers saluted to Major Raki. One of them stepped forwards. A quick conversation passed between this soldier and Major Raki.

Tim couldn't understand a single word of the conversation, because it was conducted in Stanislavian. While they were talking, he glanced at the soldier's Kalashnikov, which looked pretty cool. He wondered whether it was loaded, and decided that it must be. Then, he wondered who was on the other side of the door. Who would need to be protected by soldiers with machine guns? Someone important. But who? And why did they want to see him? Why were they interested in Timothy Malt?

The soldier stepped backwards, and opened the door. Major Raki smiled at Tim. There was something ugly and cruel about Major Raki's smile. Major Raki said, "Please, after you."

"Thanks," said Tim. He felt nervous. Nevertheless, he walked through the door. Grk trotted alongside him.

On the other side, Tim was surprised to discover another long, empty corridor. At the end, two more soldiers were standing beside another door. They must have been expecting Tim, Grk and Major Raki, because they opened the door to let them through. The three of them passed through that door, then another, and another. They passed six more soldiers, all wearing black berets and carrying Kalashnikovs. Then, they passed through one more wooden door, no different to any of the others, and entered a large room filled with sunlight and antique furniture.

A man was standing at the far end of the room. For a moment, owing to the position of the sun, Tim couldn't see the man's face. He could just see the glare of bright light and the silhouette of a big man's body. Then, the man walked towards them, and Tim got his first sight of Colonel Zinfandel. He saw a short, handsome man with a slim, straight nose and a pleasant smile. The man had black hair and lean, clean-shaven cheeks. He hurried towards Tim, and said, "Ah! You must be Timothy Malt. Is that right?"

"Yes," said Tim.

"Well, I am delighted to meet you, Timothy Malt. My name is Colonel Zinfandel."

"Hello," said Tim. "Nice to meet you. And, er, you can call me Tim. Everyone else does."

"Thank you, Tim." Colonel Zinfandel extended his hand. "Welcome to Stanislavia."

They shook hands. Colonel Zinfandel clasped Tim's shoulder, and said, "Would you like something to drink? Tea? Coffee? Orange juice?"

"Orange juice, please."

"Good choice," said Colonel Zinfandel. "I shall have the same." He nodded to Major Raki, who hurried over to the soldiers standing by the door, and whispered to them. One of the soldiers sprinted down the corridor.

Colonel Zinfandel led Tim towards the sofa. "Let's sit down. You only arrived this morning, didn't you?"

"Yes," said Tim.

"Good. Good. Tell me, what do you think of my beautiful country?"

"It seems nice," said Tim. "But I haven't seen much of it."

While they talked, Grk stood beside Tim's feet. Grk's eyes never left Colonel Zinfandel's face.

Tim and Colonel Zinfandel discussed the weather, and Tim's flight on Air Stanislavia, and the differences between London and Vilnetto. A soldier brought two tall glasses of freshly squeezed orange juice, which they drank.

I'm sorry to report that Tim liked Colonel Zinfandel very much. However, you shouldn't blame Tim too harshly for making this mistake. If you met Colonel Zinfandel for the first time, you would probably like him too. Judging him by his appearance, you would think that he looked quite nice.

Grk didn't judge people just by their appearance. He smelled them too. And Colonel Zinfandel smelled bad.

After a few minutes of chitchat, Colonel Zinfandel said, "I have something serious to tell you, Tim. Do you understand?"

"Yes. What is it?"

Colonel Zinfandel paused before continuing. A sad expression crossed his face. He said, "You have done a brave and beautiful thing by traveling to my country. You want to return this dog to his owners. Isn't that right?"

"Yes," said Tim. "She's called Natascha."

"Natascha Raffifi."

"That's right. Natascha Raffifi."

At the sound of those words, Grk's ears stood straight upright. He looked around the room. But there was no sign of his beloved mistress. Slowly, his ears drooped down again.

"I have some difficult news to tell you," said Colonel Zinfandel. "Some very difficult news." He sighed. "You see, Tim, you don't know much about the Raffifi family, do you?"

Tim shook his head.

"Do you know anything about them?"

"No," said Tim. "Nothing. Except, they own this dog."

"That's true. They are the owners of that dog. But there is something else that I must tell you about them. They are dangerous criminals. Do you understand?"

Tim was shocked. "Really? What kind of criminals?"

"The worst kind. Traitors. They have betrayed their own country."

"How?"

"I can't go into the exact details. I'm sure you understand." Colonel Zinfandel smiled. "However, I can tell you that they have spied for a foreign power, and caused untold damage to this wonderful country. Which is why they have been arrested, and put in prison."

"In prison?"

"Yes."

"Even the children? Even Natascha?"

"I'm sorry to say that the children were also involved in this appalling operation."

Tim shook his head. "It seems pretty weird."

"Weird? What do you mean by that?"

"Why would they spy against their own country?"

"That's a good question," said Colonel Zinfandel. "The answer is, I'm sorry to say, a simple one. Money. For their evil deeds, they were rewarded with a lot of money."

Tim looked at Grk. It seemed strange. If the Raffifi family were so evil, would they have such a nice dog?

Colonel Zinfandel reached forward, and put his hand on Tim's knee. "I understand that you must feel confused. Perhaps even upset. But I'm afraid that we have conclusive proof of their treachery."

"Really? What kind of proof?"

"Yesterday afternoon, Mr. and Mrs. Raffifi tried to

escape from their prison cell. They attacked a guard, causing serious injuries to him, and fled. Is that the action of innocent people?"

"No," said Tim. "I suppose not."

"Definitely not."

"And what happened? Did they escape?"

Colonel Zinfandel shook his head. "No one escapes from Vilnetto Prison. They were shot by the guards."

"Are they still alive?"

"No." Colonel Zinfandel looked sad and serious. "Unfortunately, they were killed immediately."

Tim felt sick. "What about Natascha?"

"She is still sharing a cell with her brother."

"What will happen to them?"

"They will spend the rest of their lives in prison." A smile flickered across Colonel Zinfandel's face. Then, he went back to looking serious. "You see, innocent people would never try to escape from prison. The simple fact of their attempted escape is enough to condemn them. Don't you agree?"

"I suppose so," said Tim.

"Good. I knew you would understand. You seem like an unusually intelligent young man." Colonel Zinfandel smiled. There was a peculiar glint in his eye.

Grk growled. A low, quiet growl. Tim and Colonel Zinfandel looked at Grk, who growled again. Grk's eyes never left Colonel Zinfandel's face.

"My soldiers will take care of the dog," said Colonel Zinfandel. "They will find a good home for him." He clicked his fingers.

One of the soldiers hurried across the room. Colonel Zinfandel issued a curt order to the soldier, who nodded.

The soldier extended his hand towards Tim. "Please. You give the string to me."

Tim looked at the soldier. Then he looked at Grk. Then he looked at Colonel Zinfandel. "It's okay," said Tim. "I'll take him back to England. He can live with me."

There was a long silence. Finally, Colonel Zinfandel nodded. "Very well." He stood up. "Now, let's find Sir Cuthbert. Do you know him?"

Tim shook his head. "No."

"Sir Cuthbert is the British Ambassador to Stanislavia. A charming man. He is downstairs, waiting for you. Come on, let's go downstairs."

You're probably wondering why Colonel Zinfandel was making such an effort to be nice to Tim. As we already know, Colonel Zinfandel was not a nice man. He didn't think twice about locking innocent children in high-security prisons–and, I can tell you, he did many things which were much, much worse than that. So, why was he making such an effort to be nice to Tim?

There were two reasons.

Firstly, Colonel Zinfandel needed to buy lots of guns, rockets and tanks for the Stanislavian army. As everyone knows, Britain makes some of the best guns, rockets and tanks in the world, so Colonel Zinfandel wanted to stay friends with the British. For the same reason, Colonel Zinfandel was making a great effort to stay friends with the French, the Russians, the Chinese and the Americans.

Secondly, Colonel Zinfandel wanted to be invited to lots of important conferences in foreign countries. He wanted to drive around in big cars, and shake hands with

Presidents, Prime Ministers, Kings and Queens. He wanted Stanislavia to become an important force in the United Nations. For all that to happen, he had to be friends with all the other countries, especially the big, rich and powerful ones. So, he was very careful to be good friends with the British.

He knew that Timothy Malt represented a big chance to make friends with the British. He knew that the British newspapers and television networks would be very interested in Tim's story. Colonel Zinfandel's Media Department had already been contacted by the BBC, ITV, Sky News and CNN, as well as a hundred other organizations from Europe and America. If he played his cards right, Colonel Zinfandel knew, his handsome, smiling face would be shown on televisions all around the planet, and the whole world would know his name.

19

Sir Cuthbert Winkle owned a Jaguar. Not a big cat; a big car. A chauffeur and a guard sat in the front seats. Tim, Grk and Sir Cuthbert sat in the back seats. The Jaguar drove swiftly through the streets of Vilnetto towards the British Embassy, and Sir Cuthbert said, "I have already spoken to your parents."

Tim didn't say anything. He was too busy thinking.

Sir Cuthbert continued. "They were very glad to know that you are safe. When we get to the Embassy, you can speak to them on the telephone." Sir Cuthbert smiled. "You would like to do that, wouldn't you?"

"Uh-huh," said Tim, who hadn't really been listening.

"Jolly good. Well, it's not far now. Another five minutes or so." Sir Cuthbert smiled, until he realized that Tim wasn't even looking at him. Then the smile faded slowly from Sir Cuthbert's face. He leaned back against the soft leather seat, and stared out of the window.

Sir Cuthbert didn't know much about children. He knew what they were, but he could never think of anything to say to them. So, he liked the fact that Tim didn't want to talk. Sir Cuthbert leaned back on his comfy leather seat, and daydreamed about what he would do when they arrived at the British Embassy: he would sit in his favorite armchair, drink a cup of strong tea and read a copy of yesterday's *Times.* For Sir Cuthbert, that was the worst problem with living in Vilnetto: the British papers always arrived a day late.

They drove in silence. After five minutes, they arrived at a pair of black gates in a high brick wall. A uniformed policeman was standing beside the gates. He glanced into the Jaguar, recognized the driver and the Ambassador and waved them through the gates. The Jaguar drove into the courtyard and parked outside the Embassy. The chauffeur and the guard sprang out of the front seats, hurried round to the back of the car and opened the back doors. Tim, Grk and Sir Cuthbert got out of the car.

"Thanks," said Tim to the guard, who had opened his door.

"Don't mention it," said the guard.

"This way." Sir Cuthbert beckoned to Tim. "Let's go inside and ring your parents."

They walked across the gravel, climbed some wide

stone steps and went into the house. They entered a long white hallway with high ceilings. Sir Cuthbert led Tim and Grk along the hallway, through a door and into a study. Oil paintings hung on the walls. A large wooden desk was positioned by the window, which had a view of the gardens.

Sir Cuthbert walked over to the telephone, and picked up the receiver. "Miranda? Miranda?" He knocked his knuckles against the telephone, and shouted into the receiver. "Miranda? Can you hear me?" But there was no answer. Sir Cuthbert shook his head. "I think we must be bugged. The telephones never seem to work. Excuse me, I'll be back in a minute."

Sir Cuthbert hurried out of the room to find his secretary, Miranda. When Sir Cuthbert had gone, there was no noise in the room except the ticking of an old clock.

Tim looked at Grk, who was curled on the floor with his eyes half-shut. Or perhaps his eyes were half-open. It was difficult to tell. Grk was taking the opportunity to have a nap.

Tim said, "How can you sleep at a time like this? Aren't you worried? Aren't you frightened?"

Grk opened one of his eyes, looked at Tim for a second, then closed it again.

"Okay," said Tim. "Be like that."

Five minutes later, Sir Cuthbert returned with his secretary, Miranda. She was a tall, slim woman with shoulder-length blond hair and neat black clothes. At first glance, you would assume that she was rather boring. However, there was a peculiar expression in her eyes; an expression which suggested that she was extremely amusing, intelligent and interesting but, for some reason, she had decided to hide those qualities. "Hello," said Miranda. "You must be Tim."

"Yes," said Tim. "I am."

"How nice to meet you. I'm Miranda. Sir Cuthbert's secretary. Now, do you want something to eat? And a drink?"

"No, thanks."

"Maybe a bath? A shower?"

"No, thanks," said Tim. "I'm fine."

"If you want anything, let me know. Will you do that?"

Tim nodded.

"Jolly good," said Sir Cuthbert. "So, let's ring your parents. Let them know you're safe and sound. Right?"

"Right," said Miranda. She hurried over to the telephone, and picked up the receiver.

"Um," said Tim.

They both turned to look at him.

"The thing is," said Tim, and he paused. He felt a bit nervous.

Miranda and Sir Cuthbert stared at Tim. That made him feel even more nervous.

The silence seemed to last for a long time. Tim knew that he could say, "Oh, it doesn't matter." Then, they would stop staring at him. He could talk to his parents, and get on another airplane, and go back to Britain. That would be the easiest thing to do.

Tim looked at Grk, snoozing on the thick carpet, and realized that the easiest thing isn't always the best thing. He said, "The thing is, I came here to return this dog." He pointed at Grk. "He belongs to a girl. Her name is Natascha."

"Yes," said Sir Cuthbert. His voice sounded very serious. "We know all about Natascha Raffifi. But I'm afraid you're not going to be able to see her."

"Is it true? That she's in prison?"

"I'm sorry to say that it is entirely true, yes."

"Why? What's she done?"

"According to the police, she has betrayed her country."

"But she's only a *girl*. How could she have betrayed her country?"

Sir Cuthbert paused before replying. He was trying to find the right words to say. "There's one thing that you have to understand, Tim. This isn't Britain. Things work differently here. To us, some of them may seem wrong. But that doesn't mean that we can interfere. You see, this isn't our country. These aren't our laws. We can't change them."

"So she shouldn't be in prison?"

"I don't know," said Sir Cuthbert.

"But if she was living in Britain, she wouldn't be put in prison?"

"Probably not."

"Then why can't we rescue her, and take her back to Britain?"

Sir Cuthbert smiled, and shook his head. "I'm afraid we can't interfere in the internal affairs of another country."

"Why not?"

"We just can't."

"But why not?"

Now Sir Cuthbert was getting irritated. "As I said, we can't. You'll understand when you're older."

Tim knew what those words meant. They were the words that adults used when they didn't know the answer to a question. But he also knew that there's no point arguing with an adult who uses those words. In Tim's experience, adults never admitted their own ignorance.

So Tim said, "Okay."

"Jolly good." Sir Cuthbert looked at Miranda, and nodded.

Miranda dialed a number on the telephone. "Hello. Is that Mr. Malt? This is Miranda Hopkins. That's right. Yes. I have him here." She beckoned to Tim, and passed the receiver to him.

Tim spoke into the receiver. "Hello?"

"Oh, Tim. Is it really you?" The voice on the other end of the line was Tim's father. To Tim's surprise, Mr. Malt sounded panicky, even frightened.

"I'm here," said Tim.

"Are you okay?"

"I'm fine," said Tim. "How are you?"

"We are very worried," said Mr. Malt. "Oh, God, we've been so worried. Wait a minute, your mother wants a word."

Down the phone line, Tim could hear some activity. Then his mother came onto the phone. "Tim? Tim? Are you there?"

"Yes, I'm here."

"Are you all right? Is everything all right?"

"Everything's fine," said Tim.

"Oh, thank God. And you're coming home now, aren't you?"

"Yes."

"We'll be waiting for you at the airport. Oh, and Tim?"

"Yes?"

"Bring the dog. We'll keep him. If that's what you want."

Tim was very surprised. "What about your allergy?"

"I'll do something. I'll take pills. Maybe I could even have acupuncture. That's meant to work, isn't it? If you want to keep him, you can. But you have to promise one thing in return. No more running away without telling us where you're going. Do you promise?"

"Okay," said Tim.

"Promise?"

"Yes. I promise."

"Good. Well, see you later. We'll be waiting at the airport."

"Okay."

"And Tim?"

"Yes."

"I love you. We both love you. You know that, don't you?"

"Yes," said Tim.

"See you later, then."

"Bye."

There was a click, and the phone went dead. Tim handed the receiver to Miranda. "Thanks," he said.

"There's a flight at three-thirty." Miranda smiled. "You'll be home in time for supper."

"Okay."

"You've had quite an adventure," added Sir Cuthbert. "Haven't you?"

Tim nodded.

Sir Cuthbert looked at his watch, and smiled. "We

should leave in an hour. I think we've got time for a cup of tea, don't you?"

"I'll put the kettle on," said Miranda.

They led Tim out of the study, and down the hallway to the dining room. Grk trotted behind them. When they reached the dining room, Sir Cuthbert went to find his diary, and Miranda went to make the tea. Tim knelt on the floor beside Grk.

Grk lifted his face, and sniffed Tim.

Tim whispered, "They want us to go home on the airplane. But we can't do that, can we?"

Grk licked Tim's chin.

"Uh," said Tim. "That tickles." He wiped his chin with his sleeve. "We came here to do something. We're not going home till we've done it. Okay?"

Grk's tail thumped on the thick carpet.

20

Now, Tim needed a plan. A cunning, brilliant plan to liberate Natascha Raffifi from prison, reunite her with Grk and sneak out of the country. Oh, and he wanted to liberate her brother too. So, he needed a plan to break into a high-security prison, remove two people from their cell, sneak them out of the country and travel several hundred miles back to Britain.

The problem was, Tim didn't have that kind of plan. Actually, he didn't have a plan at all.

Tim sat in the dining room for an hour. He drank the glass of orange juice that Miranda brought him, stared out of the window and tried to think of a plan. But he couldn't. He didn't have any experience in making plans like this.

Most of his life, he'd just done normal things like eating breakfast, going to school and playing on his computer. Really, he'd never had to do anything more difficult than a maths test. And maths tests, while useful if you want to learn maths, aren't much help when you're trying to break people out of prison.

While Tim tried to think, Grk lay on the carpet, and dozed. Every now and then, Grk snored. Once, he farted. Tim moved to the other side of the room until the smell went away.

After an hour, Miranda returned to the dining room, and fetched Tim and Grk. Together, they walked out of the Embassy. The Jaguar was parked on the gravel drive. A Range Rover was parked behind the Jaguar. They got into the cars, and drove away from the Embassy.

Two guards and two policemen traveled in the Range Rover. Tim, Grk, Miranda and Sir Cuthbert traveled in the Jaguar.

As they drove to Vilnetto Airport, Sir Cuthbert told Tim what would happen next. "There will be a small reception," he explained. "Nothing serious. A few photographers. Maybe a TV crew. I'm sorry, but Colonel Zinfandel is determined to use your arrival as a public relations exercise."

Miranda turned around to look at Tim. "Do you know what that means?"

"No," said Tim.

"Oh," said Sir Cuthbert. "A public relations exercise is . . . um. Well, it's like . . . You explain, Miranda."

Miranda smiled. "Public relations is the art of making yourself look good to the world. At the moment, Colonel Zinfandel doesn't look terribly good. He's deposed the

President, and stolen the country for himself. So, he'll want to use you to make himself look good."

"I don't want to make him look good," said Tim. "He's put Natascha Raffifi in prison."

Sir Cuthbert and Miranda glanced at one another. "We understand that," said Sir Cuthbert. "But we would be very grateful for your cooperation."

"Why?"

"For many reasons," said Sir Cuthbert. "Many, many reasons."

"Like what?"

Sir Cuthbert looked at Miranda. "You explain."

"The most important reason is this," said Miranda. "If we stay friends with Colonel Zinfandel, then we can ask him to help Natascha. But if we make him into our enemy, we could never ask him to do anything. In fact, if he was our enemy, he would probably do the opposite of whatever we asked. Do you understand?"

Tim understood what she said. The only problem was this: he didn't believe Colonel Zinfandel would ever free Natascha from prison. There was only one way to get her out, and it didn't involve being nice.

Tim didn't say any of this. He nodded, and smiled. "Okay. I understand."

The Jaguar and the Range Rover drove through Vilnetto. Tim stared at the crowded streets. People were shopping, or taking their children for a walk, or sitting on benches, reading newspapers, smoking cigarettes, chatting to their friends. Tim felt very strange. For the first time in his life, he was going to have to do something extraordinary. Somehow, he would have to break into a prison, liberate two children and escape from a foreign country. Meanwhile, other people were just living their lives, quite normally.

I could do that too, thought Tim. I could get on the plane, and fly back to London, and live my normal life. It would be even better than before, because Mum and Dad will let me keep Grk.

Then he chided himself for thinking like that. He would go back to his normal life—but only after he had rescued the Raffifi children from prison.

Vilnetto is a small city, so it has one small airport, which is shared by military and civilian planes. They all use the same runways. On one side of the airport, passengers get onto jets and fly to London, Paris, Istanbul, Cairo or New York. On the other side of the airport, soldiers get into helicopters or fighters, and fly around Stanislavia, protecting its borders.

The Ambassador's Jaguar and the Range Rover entered the airport through the military entrance. When the guards had checked their passports and identity cards, they drove through the gates, and followed the road to a private car park reserved for the police, the military, politicians and Very Important People.

They got out of the cars. Tim stretched his arms. The sun was shining. It felt much hotter than London. In the distance, the horizon seemed to dissolve into a shimmering haze. Across the tarmac, Tim could see a crowd of forty or fifty people. He couldn't distinguish any of their faces. However, he could see that several of them were carrying

TV cameras. Hanging above the crowd, there were long sticks, which he realized must be microphones.

Miranda saw what he was staring at. "That's the press. They're waiting for you."

"Really? For me?"

"Yes."

"Will I have to say anything?"

Miranda shook her head. "We'll take care of that. You don't have to do anything except smile. Can you do that?"

Tim nodded.

"Let's see."

Tim smiled. He didn't feel very cheerful, so his smile looked a bit fake, but it was still a smile.

"Excellent," said Miranda. "That's wonderful. Keep smiling, and you'll be a TV star before you know it."

Tim stared at the journalists. He felt nervous. Then, he noticed something else. Behind the journalists, there were three huge, long sheds. Several airplanes and helicopters were parked outside the sheds. Although they were a long way away, Tim recognized some of them. He could see a Sikorsky Sea King, a Westland Wessex and a Gazelle.

He realized what the long sheds must be: they were the hangars where the Stanislavian Air Force stored their helicopters.

In the back of his mind, Tim felt the beginnings of a plan.

It was a dangerous plan. It might have been a bad plan. But it was the only plan that he had.

Tim lifted his finger to his mouth, and bit one of his fingernails.

Sir Cuthbert leaned down, and checked his appearance

in the Range Rover's mirror. He stroked his hair, straightened his collar and adjusted his tie. Everything looked perfect. He straightened up, nodded to Miranda and smiled at Tim. "We'll have a couple of photos with the Colonel, then pop you on your plane back to London. Ready?"

Tim nodded.

"Jolly good. Let's go and face the music." Sir Cuthbert started walking briskly towards the crowd of journalists. Tim, Grk and Miranda hurried behind him. When they had walked about ten yards, Grk stopped, and sniffed the tarmac. Then he lifted his leg, and had a pee.

Tim glanced at Miranda. "No one will mind, will they?"

Miranda looked at the tiny patch of pee on the tarmac. "I don't think so. The sun is so hot, it will dry in five minutes."

Sir Cuthbert had noticed that they had stopped. He waved at them. "No dawdling, please!"

"Yes, sir," said Miranda. She winked at Tim, and they hurried after Sir Cuthbert.

Tim was starting to like Miranda.

When they reached the crowd, one of the journalists noticed Tim. He lifted his camera, and took several photographs. His movement alerted the journalist who was standing next to him, who lifted his camera too. Like a swarm of insects, all the journalists whirled around to stare at Tim. They pointed their cameras and microphones at him. They shouted questions at him. But they all shouted at the same time, so he couldn't understand what any of them were saying. Their voices mingled together like the buzzing of angry bees.

Miranda leaned down and put her mouth close to Tim's ear so only he could hear her. "Just ignore them. Pretend they're not there."

Tim looked at the journalists. How was he supposed to ignore them? There were so many of them! And they were making so much noise!

Miranda put her arm around Tim's shoulders, and hurried him towards the place where Sir Cuthbert was talking to a man in black sunglasses. It was Major Raki. When Major Raki saw them coming, he took a phone from his pocket, and made a quick call.

The journalists were making so much noise that Tim didn't hear another sound. A low, quiet sound which came from somewhere near his feet. It was the sound of Grk growling.

Major Raki finished his call, and turned to Sir Cuthbert. "Colonel Zinfandel will be here in one minute."

"Jolly good," said Sir Cuthbert. He grinned at Tim and Miranda. "This is exciting, isn't it?"

Tim nodded. Miranda smiled. Grk growled. But no one heard him.

All the journalists swiveled round, and pointed their cameras in a different direction. They had seen Colonel Zinfandel walking towards them, accompanied by ten soldiers in gleaming uniforms. In the bright sunshine, Colonel Zinfandel looked magnificent. With his broad, muscular shoulders, his long, straight nose and his confident, glittering eyes, he was the perfect picture of a great leader.

The cameras filmed Colonel Zinfandel walking across the tarmac, and reaching the small party from the British

Embassy. Major Raki saluted. Colonel Zinfandel saluted back again. Sir Cuthbert stepped forward, and opened his mouth to speak.

At that moment, Grk opened his mouth too. His pointy teeth glistened in the sunlight. He launched himself at Major Raki's ankle.

Just in time, Tim saw what was happening. He yanked the string. Inches before Grk's teeth clamped around Major Raki's ankle, the string went taut. Grk sprang backwards, and landed in a heap at Tim's feet.

Luckily, no one else noticed what had happened. They were too busy watching Colonel Zinfandel and Sir Cuthbert.

Sir Cuthbert said, "Good morning, Colonel. It's a great pleasure to see you today."

"And you, Sir Cuthbert." Colonel Zinfandel smiled. He knew that the cameras were filming every movement that he made and the microphones were recording every word that he spoke. "I understand that one of your countrymen has come to our country on a romantic mission."

"A very romantic mission," replied Sir Cuthbert. "Here he is. May I present Timothy Malt, an extraordinary young man from London."

Sir Cuthbert ushered Tim forwards. Colonel Zinfandel smiled, and said, "It is a great pleasure, Tim. I have heard so much about you. I am delighted to meet you at last."

Tim was confused. They had met already, earlier that day. But he decided that it was best to say nothing. So he did what Miranda had suggested, and just smiled.

"Welcome to our country," said Colonel Zinfandel. "Have you enjoyed what you have seen?"

Tim didn't reply. He just kept smiling.

Colonel Zinfandel didn't seem to mind. He said, "Excellent. I'm so glad to hear that."

Then, Sir Cuthbert and Colonel Zinfandel shook hands. The journalists took hundreds of pictures.

Tim noticed something strange: when Sir Cuthbert and Colonel Zinfandel shook hands, they weren't actually looking at one another. Their eyes never left the cameras.

Tim glanced at Grk. It was time to put his plan in action. He stepped backwards, and started walking across the tarmac. No one noticed that he was leaving. They were all too concerned with looking good for the cameras. He hurried across the tarmac, and headed for the hangars.

Just when Tim thought that he had escaped without anyone noticing, a heavy hand dropped onto his shoulder. He spun round to find Major Raki looking down at him.

Major Raki said, "Where are you going?"

"To the loo," replied Tim.

"I will take you."

"Not for me. For him." Tim pointed at Grk.

Major Raki and Grk looked at one another. Grk showed his teeth. Major Raki showed nothing; it was impossible to see his expression behind his dark glasses.

Tim said, "He needs a patch of grass. He's desperate."

"Very well." Major Raki nodded. "But you return immediately. Yes?"

"Yes," said Tim.

"That way." Major Raki pointed towards the perimeter fence. "You will find grass there."

"Thanks." Tim and Grk started walking in the direction that Major Raki had pointed.

After ten paces, Tim stopped, and turned round. Just as he had hoped, Major Raki wasn't watching them. He was hurrying back to Colonel Zinfandel.

Tim whispered to Grk, "Come on!"

Together, they started running. They didn't run in the direction that Major Raki had pointed them, towards the perimeter fence. Instead, they ran in the opposite direction. They ran towards the long, low hangars.

At any moment, Tim expected someone to shout and tell him to stop. He didn't know who it would be: Major Raki or Miranda or Sir Cuthbert or one of the journalists or one of the many soldiers wandering around the airport. However, to his surprise, no one shouted.

Grk bounded alongside him. Tim was still holding the piece of string tied to Grk's collar, but it was completely unnecessary. He didn't need to pull Grk. In fact, Grk pulled him.

They ran towards the nearest hangar.

The hangar was roughly the same height as a double-decker bus, and roughly the same length as fifteen buses parked in a line.

When Tim and Grk reached the end of the hangar, they stopped. Tim took a few seconds to catch his breath. Then, he sauntered slowly around the corner as if he didn't have a care in the world. He knew that you shouldn't run near military installations, or the soldiers will think that you're attacking them. Soldiers are trained to shoot first and ask questions later.

They walked around the corner, and Tim blinked. For a moment, he was so surprised, and so excited, that he couldn't even move. In his entire life, he had never seen so many helicopters. Some had been stored inside the hangar, their rotors tied down or packed away. Others were parked outside the hangar. One of them, a green Westland Wessex, was waiting on the tarmac, ready to take off. Its rotors were spinning slowly round and round. Tim could see the pilot sitting in the cabin, wearing a helmet and a military uniform.

Tim loved helicopters, but he rarely got the chance to look at them. He had been taken to three air shows by his father. They had once visited the Imperial War Museum in Duxford. Occasionally, Tim saw helicopters flying across London. Other than that, he only saw helicopters in books or on telly. He'd never done this: standing at the edge of a hangar, peering at twenty different helicopters. All different shapes. All different sizes. All different makes. All different models. None of them was particularly modern or high-tech; in fact, most of these helicopters had already been phased out of the British, French and American armies. Probably, the Stanislavian Air Force bought them secondhand for a knock-down price. But that didn't matter. They were still gleaming, beautiful helicopters in perfect working order.

Grk trotted forwards, tugging on the string tied to his collar. He looked up at Tim.

Tim nodded. Grk was right. There was no time to ogle the helicopters. They had things to do.

Most of the helicopters were unoccupied. If Tim clambered inside any of them, no one would stop him. But there was one problem with doing that: from his helicopter simulation games, Tim knew how to fly a helicopter, but he didn't know how to start the engine.

That left just one option. He would have to use the Wessex that was sitting on the tarmac with its engine running, its rotors rotating and its pilot sitting in the cabin.

Tim hurried across the tarmac. Grk jogged alongside him. They sneaked into the hangar, then doubled back and ran towards the Wessex, approaching it from behind so the pilot wouldn't see them coming.

Tim had a plan for getting the pilot out of the helicopter. There was only one problem: the plan involved Grk. For the plan to work, Grk would have to distract the pilot's attention. But how could Tim tell Grk what to do? And would Grk do it?

There was no time to worry about that. Already, his absence had probably been noticed. Miranda and Sir Cuthbert would be searching for him. Even worse, Major Raki would be searching for him.

They reached the back of the Wessex. Tim crouched down, and untied the string from Grk's collar. Above them, the tail rotor chugged round and round, making a fearsome noise. Tim looked at Grk, and pointed to a spot on the other side of the helicopter. "Go there!"

Grk stared at Tim.

"Go there! Go on, Grk! Go there!"

Grk wagged his tail. He knew that they were playing some kind of game, but he didn't understand the rules.

"Please," said Tim. "Go over there. Please, Grk. Go there! Go on!"

Grk wagged his tail even more furiously, but he didn't

move. "Tell me the rules," he seemed to be saying. "Tell me the rules, and I'll play any game you like."

Tim bit his fingernails. If he had a stick, he could have thrown it. Or a tennis ball. But he didn't.

He bit his fingernail again. If life continued being this difficult, he would soon run out of fingernails.

He realized that there was only one thing to do. It wasn't nice, but it was necessary. He picked up Grk in his arms. Grk was a small dog, so he was very light. Tim hurried along the side of the Wessex, taking care to keep out of the pilot's sight. When he reached the edge of the Wessex, he stopped, and threw Grk into the air.

Grk spun in a neat arc. His four legs scrabbled desperately. And he landed on the tarmac with a THUMP, which was swiftly followed by a SQUEAL!

Tim winced, imagining how much that must have hurt.

Grk lay on the tarmac for a moment, winded. Then he rolled over, and stared at Tim. His stare seemed to say: *I thought I liked you–but I was wrong!* After a few seconds, Grk dropped his eyes and starting licking one of his back paws.

21

Flight Lieutenant Milos Dimyat had spent twenty-three years working for the Stanislavian Air Force, but he had never seen a dog on the runway.

Until today.

Flight Lieutenant Dimyat was one of the most experienced pilots in the Stanislavian Air Force. He had flown British planes, American planes, Russian planes and French planes. He was famous for his expertise with Sikorsky helicopters. He had spent a year training with the Russian Air Force, and another year living in Texas, working with the American Air Force. He had spent most of his life in the air or hanging around airfields. And he had never seen a dog on the runway.

Until today.

He looked through the windscreen of his Westland Wessex helicopter, and saw a dog, squatting on the runway. A small dog with black and white fur, and a perky little tail.

The dog wasn't just squatting. It was licking its paws. As if it didn't have a care in the world. As if it didn't realize that it was sitting beside a large and powerful helicopter, whose whirling rotors would chop it into a hundred pieces.

Flight Lieutenant Dimyat felt extremely irritated. He stared at the dog, and hoped that it would go away.

You see, Flight Lieutenant Dimyat had a problem: he liked dogs. In fact, he loved dogs. If he hadn't liked dogs, he would have left that little mutt to get sliced into a hundred slivers by the rotors, blown away by the slipstream and crushed by the next helicopter to land on the runway. But Flight Lieutenant Dimyat and his wife owned three dogs. (A Yorkshire terrier, a whippet and a miniature schnauzer, if you're interested.) He wasn't going to let a stray dog sit on the runway and get hurt. He removed his helmet, unstrapped his seat belt and slid out of his seat. He clambered out of his helicopter. If he hadn't been so worried about the dog, he would have remembered to switch off the engine.

On the other side of the helicopter, Tim had waited and watched. He had ducked down onto the ground so he couldn't be seen. He crouched beside the helicopter's undercarriage (in other words, its wheels) and stared at Grk.

After ten or fifteen seconds, Tim saw a boot. Then another boot. He watched the boots walking across the tarmac to Grk.

"This is it," said Tim to himself. He grasped the helicopter's door and swung it open. Using all his strength, he pulled himself into the cabin.

Inside, the noise was astonishing. The engine growled. The rotors spun overhead, roaring with every rotation. Tim was deafened. His ears ached–and he'd only been inside the chopper for a couple of seconds.

He stared in terror at the cabin's interior. It was staggeringly complex. Every inch of space was covered with knobs, dials, counters and flashing lights. Tim understood what two of the dials did. That one was the altimeter; it measured your height above the ground. And that one was the speedometer; it measured how fast you were going. But what about the other hundred dials? What did they do?

Tim had no time to worry about them. Through the windscreen, he could see the pilot, who was reaching out his arms and lifting Grk off the ground. Any minute now, the pilot would turn around and see a stranger sitting in his seat.

Tim clasped the seat belt around his waist. He grasped the controls, one in each hand. He slid forward, right to the edge of his seat, and discovered that he could just reach the pedals with the tips of his toes.

Okay, thought Tim. This is it. Can I fly this thing?

Down on the runway, Flight Lieutenant Dimyat noticed a collar tied around the dog's neck. Hanging from the collar, Flight Lieutenant Dimyat could see a little round disc, the size of a small coin, with some words engraved on it. This dog wasn't a stray. It had an owner. Someone cared about it. Someone loved it. Flight Lieutenant Dimyat decided that it was his duty to return this dog to its owner.

He reached down, put his hands around the dog and picked it up.

At that moment, he heard an extraordinary noise. It sounded as if the rotors of his helicopter had started whirring faster. That was impossible. Nevertheless, Flight Lieutenant Dimyat turned around. When he saw the helicopter, his mouth dropped open.

The rotors *were* going faster. Not only that: he could see someone sitting inside the helicopter. Sitting in *his* seat. Wearing *his* seat belt. *Stealing his helicopter!*

Flight Lieutenant Dimyat blinked, and stared through the windscreen. The person in his seat looked tiny. His helicopter was being stolen by a midget!

The rotors whirled faster and faster. In a few seconds, the chopper would have enough power to take off.

Like every other officer in the Stanislavian Army and Air Force, Flight Lieutenant Dimyat carried a gun. He couldn't grab his pistol immediately, because he had a dog in his arms. So he dropped the dog, and reached for his pistol.

For the second time in one day, Grk got dropped on concrete.

The first time that Grk got dropped on concrete, he had been confused, upset and disappointed. The second time that Grk got dropped on concrete, he was furious.

He whirled around, and bit the nearest ankle that he could see.

Flight Lieutenant Dimyat pointed his pistol at the midget who was stealing his helicopter.

His finger tightened on the trigger.

At that moment, he felt a terrible pain in his left ankle. He was so surprised that he dropped the pistol. It flew out of his hand, and skidded across the tarmac.

He looked down. The dog was looking up at him. On its face, the dog seemed to have a self-satisfied smile.

Flight Lieutenant Dimyat said, "You little . . ."

Before Flight Lieutenant Dimyat could finish the sentence, the dog whirled round and sprinted away from him, heading for the helicopter. The door opened for a moment. The dog leaped inside. The door slammed shut.

As soon as the door shut, the helicopter shuddered. It wobbled. And lifted off the ground.

Flight Lieutenant Dimyat felt sick. Now he realized what was going on. It was a plot. A devilish plot to make him look like an idiot. His helicopter was being stolen by a midget and a dog!

He didn't stop to think. If he had been thinking clearly, he would have sprinted across the tarmac, grabbed his gun and fired a couple of shots into the helicopter's engine. At this short range, he would have disabled the engine, and the helicopter would have glided safely back onto the runway.

But Flight Lieutenant Dimyat was too angry to think clearly. So he ran straight at the helicopter, which was lifting off the runway. It lifted a foot into the air. Flight Lieutenant Dimyat ran faster. The helicopter lifted another foot into the air . . . and another . . . Just before the helicopter soared into the sky, Flight Lieutenant Dimyat threw himself at the undercarriage, and grabbed one of the wheels.

• • •

Here is a question for you. Can you do all these things at the same time?

Rub your tummy with your left hand.

Pat your head with your right hand.

Tap both your feet in time to some music.

If you can't, then don't even think about trying to fly a helicopter.

When you fly a helicopter, you have to do lots of things at the same time. Some of them are obvious. You have to peer out of the window, and check that you're not going to hit anything. You have to look out for trees, pylons, wires, buildings, birds, planes and other helicopters. You have to watch all the instruments on your control panel which say how high you are, how fast you're going and how much fuel you have.

At the same time, you have to use both your hands and both your feet.

Your feet control the pedals. If you push the left-hand pedal, you turn to the left. If you push the right-hand pedal, you turn to the right.

Meanwhile, your left hand controls a lever called the collective control stick. It makes the helicopter go up and down.

And your right hand? That controls another lever, which you find between your knees. It is called the cyclic control stick, and it makes the helicopter move forwards, backwards and to either side.

Does that sound complicated? Yes? Well, it is complicated. Flying a helicopter is fiendishly complicated. Don't even bother trying unless you have a high IQ, strong muscles in your arms and legs, a good teacher and many hours free for practicing.

Fortunately for Tim, he had spent many, many hours playing helicopter simulation games on his computer. He knew all about the cyclic control stick, the collective control stick and the pedals. Although he had never actually flown a helicopter, he knew exactly what to do.

He pushed the cyclic control stick forwards, and the helicopter lurched towards the clouds. He pushed the left-hand pedal, and the helicopter whirled around to the left. He pulled back the collective control stick, and the helicopter lifted into the air.

He couldn't believe that everything was going so well.

Then he looked down, and saw a man hanging from one of the wheels.

22

On the other side of the airfield, Colonel Zinfandel and Sir Cuthbert Winkle were posing for the cameras. Both of them had big smiles on their faces. They were taking turns to answer questions from journalists.

One of the journalists said, "Colonel Zinfandel, do you have any plans to visit Great Britain?"

Colonel Zinfandel grinned. "I have always wanted to visit London, and take tea with the Queen. But I am still waiting for my invitation."

"You shouldn't have to wait too long," said Sir Cuthbert.

The journalist turned her attention to the British Ambassador. "Does that mean, Sir Cuthbert, that Colonel

Zinfandel will soon be receiving an invitation to take tea with the Queen?"

"I can't make any guarantees," said Sir Cuthbert. "But I hope that the friendship between our countries will be strong and fruitful."

Colonel Zinfandel looked at the crowd of journalists. "Are there any more questions?"

Several journalists put their hands in the air. Colonel Zinfandel pointed at one of them. "Yes, you. The blond lady. Yes. What is your question?"

The journalist was a blond woman who hadn't spoken before. She spoke English with a strong accent. She said, "I am writer for woman magazine, *House and Home.* I have one question. When will English boy be speaking? Timothy Malt. My readers like to hear from him."

Colonel Zinfandel nodded. "Of course, yes, he will speak now. You can ask him all the questions that you want. Sir Cuthbert?"

"Yes, yes," said Sir Cuthbert. "Jolly good idea. Let's get Tim to answer some questions." He looked around, but he couldn't see any sign of Tim. So he looked at Miranda. "Where is he?"

Miranda shrugged her shoulders. "He took the dog for a walk."

"Took the dog for a walk? During a press conference?" Sir Cuthbert gritted his teeth. "Find him, Miranda. And quickly."

"Yes, sir," said Miranda. She pushed through the crowd, and hurried across the runway in the direction that Tim had gone.

Major Raki followed her.

• • •

When Miranda had gone, Sir Cuthbert smiled at the journalists. "Tim has sneaked off for a moment. You know what small boys are like. Never happy to sit still. He'll be here in a second. Before that, do we have any other questions?"

Several journalists put their hands up.

"Yes." Sir Cuthbert pointed at one of the journalists. "You. What's your question?"

The journalist opened his mouth, but didn't speak. He just stared at something behind Sir Cuthbert's head.

"Come on, come on," said Sir Cuthbert. "Do you want to ask a question or not?"

The journalist's mouth opened even wider, but he still didn't speak.

At that moment, Sir Cuthbert heard a loud buzzing noise which seemed to be coming from behind him. It sounded as if a huge bee was buzzing straight at his head. He turned round to see what was making that terrible din. This is what he saw: on the other side of the runway, near the hangars, a helicopter was lifting into the sky. The helicopter was a green Westland Wessex, and something seemed to be dangling from one of its wheels.

A gasp went up from the crowd as the helicopter dived to the left, and plunged towards the ground.

There was another collective gasp as the helicopter lurched to the right, and lifted into the air.

If the helicopter had been human, you would have guessed that it had drunk three bottles of wine for lunch.

As the helicopter wobbled and soared closer to the

crowd of journalists, Colonel Zinfandel said, "But . . . But . . . But that's my helicopter!"

Sir Cuthbert stared at him in astonishment. "Your helicopter?"

"Yes. That's my private helicopter!"

"Really? Extraordinary. And who's that hanging from the undercarriage?"

For a second, Colonel Zinfandel was too shocked to speak. Then he said in a low, angry voice, "That is my pilot."

"Funny way to fly a chopper," said Sir Cuthbert. "Hanging from the undercarriage. Most unconventional!"

Colonel Zinfandel hissed, "I do not think that he is flying the helicopter."

"Oh, really?" Sir Cuthbert looked confused. "Then who is?"

"I do not know," said Colonel Zinfandel. "But I shall find out. And when I find them, I shall . . ."

He left the rest of the sentence unspoken, as if he was going to do something so horrible that it couldn't be put into words.

Colonel Zinfandel and Sir Cuthbert stood side by side, watching the helicopter as it flew closer to them, swooping dramatically from side to side. Each swoop threatened to dislodge the man hanging from the undercarriage, who was hurled from left to right. His legs scrabbled desperately, as if he was trying to find a foothold in the empty air.

The crowd of journalists were very excited. A missing boy from London, a dog, a drunk helicopter with a man hanging from the undercarriage–this story got better and better! The journalists frantically scribbled in their notebooks, and filmed with their cameras and rang their editors. HOLD THE FRONT PAGE!

As the helicopter flew closer, it plummeted towards the ground. Seconds before smashing into the runway, the helicopter's nose lifted, and swung to the left, veering dangerously close to the journalists. Most of them ducked. The helicopter skidded over their heads, its rotors thudding round and round with an appalling roar.

The helicopter flew so low that the people on the ground could see inside the cockpit. They could see the features of the pilot. Their jaws dropped as they recognized him.

"Oh, gosh," blurted Sir Cuthbert. "That's him! That's Timothy Malt!"

"Timothy Malt," repeated Colonel Zinfandel, in a low, ominous tone.

Sir Cuthbert shouted at the top of his voice: "Timothy! Timothy! What are you doing? Put that thing down now!"

Even if Timothy Malt had been able to hear Sir Cuthbert, he wouldn't have taken any notice. He was concentrating too hard on flying the helicopter. Sweat dripped down his forehead. His arms ached. Piloting the helicopter was like riding a wild animal. Tim felt like a cowboy on a crazy horse, a bucking bronco, which danced from side to side, trying to throw off its rider.

He tried to swoop down near the runway. The first time, he missed his target, and nearly crashed into the crowd of journalists. So he accelerated upwards again. The helicopter tipped back. Grk fell against the seat, and yelped. Tim pushed the left-hand pedal, dipped the control stick and veered towards the ground.

This time, he aimed for an empty patch of grass. The helicopter swung downwards. Tim knew that he had to go as close to the ground as possible, then immediately soar into the air again.

He swooped down to the ground, giving his passenger a chance to jump. His passenger took the chance. Flight Lieutenant Dimyat let go, and plunged towards the grass. The drop was only five or six feet. Flight Lieutenant Dimyat had done lots of parachute training, so he knew how to land on the earth without hurting himself. Both his feet hit the ground at the same time; then he rolled over, cushioning himself against the blow.

Timothy had already pulled back the collective control stick. The helicopter shot into the sky.

Major Raki raised his gun and prepared to fire.

When the helicopter was flying towards the crowd of journalists, Major Raki had seen immediately who was flying it. He knew how to stop them. He unholstered his pistol, and held it with both hands to ensure that he got a steady shot.

He took aim. With one good shot, he would cripple the helicopter's engine. It would tumble to the ground. If he was lucky, it might even explode in a huge ball of flame. At the thought of that, Major Raki's mouth lifted in a cruel smile. He aimed the gun. The helicopter lifted into the sky, and Major Raki tightened his finger on the trigger.

As Major Raki pulled the trigger, he was knocked sideways. The bullet shot out of his gun, flew across the runway and smacked harmlessly into the side of the hangar.

Major Raki rolled over, and took aim again. But he was too late. The helicopter had already risen into the sky, and he couldn't get a good shot.

So he turned around, and pointed his gun at the person who had knocked him sideways.

Miranda didn't raise her hands in the air. Nor did she look frightened or beg for mercy. Instead, she smiled. "If I were you, I'd put the gun down."

Major Raki snarled, "And why should I do that?"

"Because you don't want to shoot me."

"And why not?"

"Because I am a representative of the British Government. If you fire a shot at me, you are effectively declaring war on Great Britain. How would your Colonel Zinfandel feel about that?"

Major Raki knew that she was right. But he wasn't going to give her the satisfaction of saying so. He slid his pistol into its holster, and strolled past Miranda without even looking at her.

He had been made to look stupid by a woman. Major Raki didn't like being made to look stupid, and he didn't like women. One day, he promised himself, he would have his revenge on this irritating Englishwoman. One day soon.

23

It was lucky that Tim had a good memory. Otherwise, the helicopter would have been completely useless. He would have flown round and round in circles, not knowing where to go.

But he remembered his route from Vilnetto Airport to the center of the city: they had driven along a motorway, and passed the prison where the Raffifi children were confined. High in the sky, Tim hovered the helicopter, and peered through the windscreen.

Grk pressed his nose against the glass, and stared through the window. It was the first time that Grk had ever flown in a helicopter, and he seemed to be enjoying the experience.

Down below, hundreds of feet under them, Grk and Tim could see the landscape, spread out like a map. From here, everything looked tiny. The cars looked like matchboxes. Buildings looked like books. People's heads looked like apple pips.

There, leading away from the airport like a strip of gray ribbon, Tim could see the motorway. On the horizon, he could see a patch of brown, dirty smog. That must be the center of Vilnetto. If he followed the motorway, he would find the prison. He turned the helicopter, flew over to the motorway and followed it towards the city.

Helicopters travel very fast.

The crowd of journalists watched the helicopter as it soared into the sky, hovered for a few seconds, then headed in the direction of Vilnetto. After a minute, the helicopter disappeared over the horizon.

Immediately, the journalists ran to their cars. They wanted to follow the helicopter into the city, and see where it would go next.

At the same time, Colonel Zinfandel was shouting furiously at Major Raki.

Colonel Zinfandel's face was bright red. If his cheeks turned any redder, they would probably explode. He was angry for three reasons. Firstly, his helicopter had been stolen. Secondly, he had been made to look like an idiot. Thirdly, he had been made to look like an idiot *by a little boy.*

Major Raki nodded, but didn't say a single word. When Colonel Zinfandel was angry, it was sensible to keep quiet.

Colonel Zinfandel issued a series of orders. He wanted the helicopter stopped. He wanted the boy brought to him. He wanted to punish the boy. Really punish him so he suffered a lot of horrible pain. Colonel Zinfandel stared at Major Raki, and whispered, "After this, no one will ever try to steal one of my helicopters again."

"No, sir."

"Because they will know the consequences."

"Yes, sir."

"Do you understand what I'm saying?"

Major Raki nodded. "I understand precisely, sir."

"Then what are you waiting for?"

Major Raki clicked his heels together, saluted and hurried across the runway.

A few feet away, Sir Cuthbert was interrogating Miranda.

"It just doesn't make any sense," said Sir Cuthbert. "That little boy–flying a helicopter. Why would he do that? And how could he do that? How could he possibly know how to fly a helicopter?"

"I don't know, sir," replied Miranda.

"Extraordinary," muttered Sir Cuthbert.

"Yes, sir."

Sir Cuthbert glanced at Miranda. "Do you know how to fly a helicopter?"

"No, sir."

"Nor do I. So how does a little boy?" Sir Cuthbert frowned. "You don't think he's a spy, do you?"

"That's certainly possible, sir."

"If he is, I hope he's one of ours."

"Yes, sir."

Sir Cuthbert nodded to himself. "We could use a few chaps like him."

"Twelve-year-old boys who can fly helicopters?"

"They'd certainly be useful, wouldn't they?"

"I suppose they would, sir."

"Jolly useful."

"Shall I write a memo to the Head of the Secret Service?"

"Good idea," said Sir Cuthbert. Then the smile faded from his face. "Oh, gosh. What's the Foreign Secretary going to say?"

"About what, sir?"

"We've lost that little boy, haven't we? He was supposed to get on that plane. He was supposed to fly back to London and meet his parents. They're going to be waiting at Heathrow Airport. Oh, dear. I think the Foreign Secretary is going to be furious." Sir Cuthbert clapped his hands together. "Come on, Miranda. This is no time for standing around. We've got to find him."

"Yes, sir," said Miranda. "And how are we going to do that, sir?"

"I have an idea," said Sir Cuthbert. "Follow me."

Together, they hurried across the runway towards Colonel Zinfandel.

They arrived just as Major Raki was leaving. Colonel Zinfandel was still red-faced and furious. Anyone could see that this wasn't the best time to have a conversation with him. But Sir Cuthbert didn't have any choice. Rather nervously, Sir Cuthbert said, "Ah, Colonel Zinfandel. How are you?"

"Not good," replied Colonel Zinfandel. "Not good at all."

"I'm terribly sorry to hear that," said Sir Cuthbert. "The thing is, we have a little problem. That boy, Timothy Malt. You remember him? Of course you do. Well, somehow we have to get him back to England. You see, his parents are waiting for him, and the Foreign Secretary will be terribly upset if they have to wait too long."

"Yes, you are right," said Colonel Zinfandel. "Timothy Malt is a problem. A big problem. Luckily, I have a perfect solution to this problem."

"Oh, yes? Really?"

"Really."

"Tremendous," said Sir Cuthbert. "And what exactly is your solution?"

"One of my fighter planes will fly after the helicopter and shoot it down with a missile. Little Timothy Malt will die in a big explosion." Colonel Zinfandel chuckled. Then he remembered how angry he was, and he stopped chuckling immediately.

Sir Cuthbert said, "Er, well. Um. Actually, I don't think that's such a good idea."

"It is a very good idea," replied Colonel Zinfandel.

"No, no," said Sir Cuthbert. "I have to warn you not to endanger that boy. If any harm comes to that boy, you will feel the full force of Her Majesty's Government's displeasure."

Colonel Zinfandel drew himself up to his full height.

In his pride and anger, Colonel Zinfandel was an impressive man. He spat out his words: "But he has stolen one of my helicopters!"

"That may be so," said Sir Cuthbert. "Nevertheless, he is a British citizen. He will be accorded every protection by the Government of the United Kingdom."

"Every protection?"

"Yes."

Colonel Zinfandel smiled. "Really? And if I kill him with a missile? Then what will you do?"

"We will do whatever is necessary," replied Sir Cuthbert.

"Do what you like." With those words, Colonel Zinfandel turned on his heel, and stalked away.

"Oh, my goodness," said Sir Cuthbert. He watched the retreating figure of Colonel Zinfandel. "Oh, kittens. What are we going to do now?"

"I don't know, sir." Miranda pointed across the runway. "But we'd better do something fast. Look!"

Sir Cuthbert looked in the direction that Miranda was pointing.

On the other side of the runway, two fighter jets were accelerating along the runway. Their engines roared. One after another, they shot into the sky. They rocketed away from the airport, flying in the direction that the helicopter had already gone.

"Oh, gosh." Sir Cuthbert stared at the fighters. "What are they going to do?"

"They're going to shoot him down, sir," said Miranda.

"Stop them! Stop them!"

"Yes, sir," said Miranda. She turned around, and ran

towards the car park to where the Embassy's cars were parked.

Left alone, Sir Cuthbert shook his head. He watched two more fighter jets taxi along the runway. "Oh, golly. Oh, trumpets," muttered Sir Cuthbert. "What's the Foreign Secretary going to say now?"

24

With every minute that Tim spent in the air, his flying improved. He flew more smoothly, and without wobbling so much. Flying a real helicopter, he realized, isn't very different to flying a helicopter simulator on a computer.

Of course, there is one big difference. If you crash a helicopter on your computer, you can press a button, and start the level again with another helicopter, a full tank of petrol, loads of ammunition and a nice new body. If you crash a real helicopter, you don't get any second chances. But Tim tried not to think about that.

He flew about five hundred feet above the earth. If he had been flying near pylons, tower blocks or skyscrapers, five hundred feet would have been too low. But he was flying above a motorway which cut through the middle of the countryside, and the only structures were farmhouses, fences and sheds.

On the horizon, he saw a huge squat gray building, surrounded by high walls. He recognized it. That was the prison which had been pointed out by the driver. That was where he would find the Raffifi children. Tim pressed down on the left-hand pedal, tilting the helicopter gently to the left, and headed towards the prison.

He was flying fast. After three or four minutes, he buzzed over the prison. Below him, he could see the outer walls, tipped with coils of barbed wire.

The prison was protected like a fortress: after the first high wall, there was a moat, then two more walls. Tim flew over the walls, looking for somewhere to land.

Inside the prison, every window had iron bars over the glass. Every door was locked. Every corridor was guarded by two uniformed guards, and every guard carried a gun, a truncheon and three pairs of handcuffs. No one had ever escaped from Vilnetto Prison. Luckily, Tim didn't know that. Otherwise, he might have turned the helicopter around, and flown in the opposite direction.

Tim hovered over the courtyard. That looked like a good place to land. Then, he remembered something.

He didn't know how to land.

Tim knew how to fly a helicopter. On his computer, he could fire missiles and drop bombs. He could dodge round tower blocks and skim round trees and fight other helicopters. However, he had no idea how to land.

"Hold on," he said to Grk. "This might be tricky."

Grk looked out of the window, and wagged his tail. He was having fun.

Tim concentrated very hard. Using the pedals and the levers, he hovered lower and lower. In the courtyard, he could see a few prisoners and a few guards, staring into the air. Staring at him. Tim didn't have time to worry about them. He struggled with the controls.

Grk barked.

"Okay, okay," said Tim. "Hold on."

Grk barked again. He had seen two small figures in the corner of the yard. Grk recognized the shape of those figures. He barked at them as loudly as he could, hoping that they would wave back at him. They didn't, so he barked even louder.

Tim bent the collective control stick forwards. The helicopter's nose tipped down, and they plunged towards the ground. Grk slid off the seat, and banged against the windscreen. He squeaked.

The ground rushed towards them.

Tim pulled the collective control stick back again. The helicopter skidded across the courtyard, just a foot or two above the concrete. People ran for their lives.

Grk scuttled back down the helicopter, bounced off the seat and hit his head against Tim's elbow, knocking the control stick forwards.

"No!" shouted Tim.

But it was too late. The helicopter plunged towards the ground. Concrete filled the windscreen. At the last moment, just before they crashed, Tim yanked back the control stick. The helicopter screamed upwards. Another few inches, and the helicopter would have been fine. It almost missed the ground. Almost, but not quite. Its tail scraped against the concrete, splintered, and broke into pieces. The helicopter tipped over sideways, wobbled and smashed into the wall.

All around the courtyard, guards and prisoners stood stock still, rooted to the spot by shock.

Glass and metal splattered through the air. Oil splashed across the concrete. Smoke billowed out of the fuel tank. Flames licked the mangled rotors.

Two figures struggled out of the wreckage. One of them, a small boy, wiped his face with his hands. The other, a little dog, shook himself.

Then the helicopter exploded in a bright ball of flame, and the two figures disappeared in a cloud of black smoke.

A helicopter has a big fuel tank. A Westland Wessex can carry about two thousand liters of petrol in its tank. That's the same as forty cars. When forty cars explode, they make a big bang.

All over the prison, people heard the explosion. The guards panicked. The prisoners got excited. All of them assumed that someone was blowing up the prison.

In his office, the Prison Governor picked up his red telephone, and called for reinforcements.

In the courtyard, the helicopter was burning fiercely. Bright flames caressed the wreckage. Glass cracked and popped. Metal fizzed and buckled. A tower of smoke lifted into the air, like a signal to everyone for miles around.

A military helicopter is packed with weapons and ammunition. The heat of the explosion acted like a trigger, igniting every weapon. Missiles shot out of the helicopter's wreckage. Bullets pinged in every direction. Sparks cascaded. Hot glass fizzed. Trails of smoke littered the sky. It looked like a firework display on a rich man's birthday.

All around the prison, bullets and missiles exploded. Bars broke off windows. Holes opened in the walls. Fires started. Flames licked the brickwork.

All around the prison, the prisoners realized that this was their big chance: if they jumped through the holes in the walls, they would be free. So, they started jumping.

Tim's hair was burnt. His face was black. Smoke rose from smoldering holes in his clothes. He staggered to his feet, and looked around for Grk.

Behind him, he saw the crumpled metal and shattered glass which had once been a helicopter. Through the flames, he could see a hole in the wall: the explosion must have blown through the bricks. But there was no sign of Grk.

He turned round, and looked the other way.

There! There he was! Streaking across the courtyard!

Before the explosion, Grk's fur had been black and white. Now, it was black all over. He looked like he had been barbecued. But he was alive, and free, and he could still run very fast. His tongue was hanging out. He was crazy with excitement and anticipation.

Grk sprinted across the courtyard, heading for two small figures who were standing in the corner: a boy and a girl. When he reached them, he leaped off the ground, and hurled himself into the girl's arms.

Natascha Raffifi was so shocked that she couldn't speak. But she didn't need to say anything: she just hugged

Grk. A pair of tears collected in the corners of her eyes, and trickled down her cheeks. Grk lifted his head. With his little pink tongue, he licked away her tears.

Ten seconds later, Tim arrived. He looked at the boy and the girl. He felt embarrassed and awkward. He had traveled for hundreds of miles to meet these people–and now, having met them, he couldn't think of anything to say.

Perhaps, he thought, I should just turn round and go home without saying anything.

But that would have been silly. So he smiled and said, "Hello."

The two Raffifi children stared at him. Both of them looked very confused. You can understand why. They had been taking their usual midafternoon walk around the prison courtyard when a helicopter fell out of the sky, crashed into a wall and exploded into flames. As if that wasn't enough, two blackened figures had emerged from the wreckage. One of them was their dog, and the other was a small boy with freckles and an English accent. Does that kind of thing happen to you every day? If it does, your life is a lot more exciting than mine.

Max was the first to recover from the shock. He said, "Who are you?"

"I've come to return your dog," said Tim. "He is your dog, isn't he?"

Tim's question didn't really need an answer. If you saw Grk, you would have known immediately that he had found his owners. He was sitting in Natascha's arms, running his tongue over her face, as if her cheeks were covered with chocolate.

At that moment, two fighter planes roared over the prison, flying low. They spotted the plume of smoke, and circled overhead.

Tim realized that the pilots would see exactly what was happening. They would be radioing for reinforcements. They might even be preparing to drop a bomb or fire some missiles. He looked around the courtyard. Three guards were standing in the left-hand corner. One of them was speaking into a walkie-talkie.

"Okay," said Tim. "How are we going to get out of here?"

25

Max and Natascha stared at Tim. Then they looked at one another, and started arguing furiously in Stanislavian.

Tim couldn't understand what they were saying. He looked around the courtyard. In the first few moments after the explosion, the guards and the prisoners had been too shocked to move. Now, they were picking themselves up. The guards were regrouping. They were grown men with guns and truncheons. Tim and the Raffifi children would be powerless against them.

Tim said, "Excuse me?"

Neither of the Raffifi children took any notice. They probably didn't even hear him. A little louder, Tim said, "Hello? Hello? Remember me?"

That time, the Raffifi children heard him, but they took no notice. They just continued arguing amongst themselves. So Tim raised both of his hands and shouted, "SHUT UP!"

The two children stopped their argument, and stared at him. Tim said, "Sorry for shouting. But there's no time to argue. We have to get out of here *right now*!"

Max shook his head. "No. That is not possible."

"Why not?"

"Because our parents are also locked in this prison. We cannot leave without them."

Tim lifted his left hand to his mouth, and bit his fingernail. He remembered what Colonel Zinfandel had said: Max's parents were dead. Mr. and Mrs. Raffifi had been shot while trying to escape from the prison.

At that moment, Tim was confronted with a terrible choice. Should he admit what he knew? He couldn't do that; he couldn't tell these two children that their parents had been murdered. So, should he pretend that he didn't know the truth? Then, Max and Natascha would insist on staying in the prison to find their parents, and they would be killed too. Their deaths would be pointless. They would die trying to save two people who were already dead.

Tim said, "We'll never find your parents in this place. With any luck, they'll escape on their own. We have to get out of here, and we have to do it right now."

Natascha and Max looked at one another. Their lives had been much more complicated than Tim's. Even so, this was one of the most difficult decisions that they had ever been forced to make.

Max stared at Tim. "Who are you? What's your name?"

Tim looked around the courtyard. One of the guards had pulled out a gun. Another had taken out his truncheon. Tim said, "My name's Timothy Malt. You can call me Tim. But that doesn't matter. We just have to get out of here."

"Where are you from? England?"

"Yes."

"And how old are you?"

"Twelve."

Max looked at Natascha. "He's the same age as you."

Natascha said, "So what?"

"He's only a kid. I'm not going to take orders from a kid."

"My age doesn't matter," said Tim. "What matters is whether I'm right or wrong."

Max shook his head. "The same age as my kid sister! Do you really expect me to take orders from someone who's twelve?"

"I'm not ordering you to do anything," said Tim. "I'm just saying, we have to get out of here. Right now."

Max replied, "But I don't know anything about you. You might be a liar. Or a spy."

"I'm not."

"That's what you say. But how do I know if you're telling the truth? Why should I trust you?"

"He brought Grk," interrupted Natascha. "If he did that, I'm happy to trust him." She lowered her beloved dog to the ground. Grk spun round and barked joyfully. "Come on," said Natascha, and held out her hand to Tim. "Let's go. If Max wants to stay here, he can."

Tim grabbed Natascha's hand. Together, they ran

towards the helicopter, which was still gushing plumes of black smoke.

Max watched them go.

What should he do? Try to fight three armed guards? Or trust a twelve-year-old boy with freckles who he had never seen before?

He looked around the courtyard, and gazed at the high walls. As far as he knew, his parents were still locked in one of those cells, confined behind those barred windows.

Leaving them felt like the worst thing that he had ever done. But he knew that he had to do it. He had no choice.

Looking at the high walls, he spoke a few silent words. He made a solemn promise. "I promise," he said, "I will come back and get you. Whatever it takes, Mother and Father, I shall be back for you."

Although Max spoke these words in the privacy of his own mind, he heard them as clearly as if he had yelled them at the top of his voice.

Then he sprinted after the others.

26

The prison was a massive building, which held more than three thousand prisoners. Some were murderers. Others were thieves. Some hadn't paid their taxes. Others had done nothing worse than criticize Colonel Zinfandel.

When Colonel Zinfandel took over the country, he sent his soldiers to arrest his enemies, handcuff them, load them into military vans and toss them into prison. Colonel Zinfandel had a lot of enemies, so the prison was extremely crowded.

Now, after the explosion, all the prisoners had the same thought: they wanted to be free. Murderers, thieves, tax dodgers, enemies of Colonel Zinfandel and all the rest–they wanted freedom. They were running through the corridors, hollering and shouting, looking for an exit, searching for a hole in the wall that would lead to freedom.

What about the guards? Weren't they supposed to guarding the prisoners?

Most of the guards were sensible men. They knew when they were beaten. Being a guard was just their job, and they didn't want to be killed doing it. So they locked themselves in the cells, and waited for the reinforcements to arrive.

"This way," said Tim. "Follow me."

He led the Raffifi family across the courtyard to the smoldering helicopter. Flames flickered on the cracked metal, and black smoke coiled into the sky. The air was hot. They felt the heat roasting their cheeks and foreheads.

"Down here," said Tim. "Quick! We don't have much time."

Max peered through the smog. "Where are you taking us?"

"Out of this place," said Tim, and ushered Natascha forwards.

With each step, the heat intensified. It was like being cooked. Tim's cheeks felt fried. Under his feet, embers scorched his soles. When he stopped for a moment to check that the others were following, his shoes started melting; he looked down, and saw little patches of steam rising around his feet. He started shuffling around, jogging on the spot. If he stood still, his molten soles would glue him to the ground.

"Through that hole," he hissed to Natascha, and

pointed to a gap in the bricks. The explosion had blown a hole through the prison's wall. On the other side, Tim remembered from flying over the prison, there would be a wall, then the bridge over the moat, then another wall. After that, they would be free.

Grk was dancing around like a puppet whose strings are all being pulled at once. He had no shoes, so the embers burnt his paws. When Natascha eased through the hole in the wall, Grk sprang gratefully after her. On the other side, Natascha brushed the dust and loose chunks of brick from her dress. Grk lay at her feet and licked his hot paws, trying to cool them down with his saliva.

Max squeezed through the hole. Tim jumped down last. He looked around. They were standing in a narrow passageway. On either side, high, windowless walls stretched towards the sky.

Max looked up and down the passageway. "Which way? That way? Or that way?"

Tim didn't know which way to go: both ends of the passageway looked exactly the same. However, before he could answer, the decision was made for him. A huge man appeared at one end of the passage. His legs were as thick as telegraph poles, and his massive hands looked like bunches of pink bananas. He was dressed in a guard's uniform, and carrying a truncheon. He started running towards the children.

"Oh, no," whispered Natascha. She stared at the guard in horror. "What do we do now?"

The guard sprinted towards them, waving his truncheon and running as fast as his legs would go.

"I don't know," said Tim. "Stand and fight? Or run?"

"Stand and fight," said Max. He put up his fists, and waited for the guard to reach them.

At Natascha's feet, Grk licked his lips, then started growling. If they were going to fight, he was ready!

Tim didn't like fighting. But he had no desire to look like a coward. So he put up his fists too, and waited.

The guard ran towards them. When he reached the children, he didn't stop. He continued running as quickly as he could, and sprinted straight past them.

The children looked at one another, surprised and confused.

Another man charged around the corner and started running towards the children. He was shouting and hollering. "Come back! Come back here!" In his right hand, he had a big stick, which he waved round and round his head. "Come back here! You fat coward! Come here and let me beat you!"

Behind him, another man appeared. Then another. Then two more. Five more. Ten more. Every one of the men was carrying a makeshift weapon: a stick, the leg of a chair, a twisted metal bar. They were prisoners who had suffered horribly at the hands of this guard. Now, they were determined to take their revenge.

They charged past the children, and chased the guard down the passageway.

Max and Natascha looked at one another, and started excitedly discussing what had happened.

"There's no time for talking," interrupted Tim. "Follow me!"

He hurried after the crowd of men. Natascha and Grk followed him. After a moment's hesitation, so did Max.

They ran down the passageway, turned left, then right, and entered a second courtyard. A stream of prisoners were running in the same direction: towards a wooden gate which had been broken open, and now hung off its hinges.

"They seem to know where they're going," said Tim. "Let's follow them. Through that gate. Okay?"

Max and Natascha nodded.

The children joined the prisoners, and streamed through the gate. On the other side, the children and the prisoners hurried down the road. They charged over the bridge which crossed the moat.

After the bridge, the road continued for a few more feet, then stopped. A huge metal gate blocked the route. You might be able to break open this gate–but only if you were driving a tank or a bulldozer.

On the other side of the gate, there was freedom. On this side, angry men chanted and jeered, demanding that the gate was opened. Every second, more men joined the crowd. Among them, Tim and the Raffifi children felt very nervous.

Above the gate, there was an observation tower. Day and night, two guards stood in this tower, watching the walls through binoculars, checking that no one tried to escape. Now, the two guards were staring down at the crowd of men. Both guards held pistols in their hands. A ladder led up to the tower, but no one dared climb it; everyone knew that the guards would shoot any prisoner who climbed further than the first rung.

Tim looked at the guards, then the crowd. The prisoners were dirty, and many of them looked vicious. He wondered how many of these men were murderers. How many had robbed banks? How many had blown up buildings? They were already angry. What would they do when they got angrier? Would they fight? Would they kill? For a second, Tim remembered his bedroom, his computer and the packets of Hula Hoops in the kitchen cupboard. What was he doing here? Why wasn't he sitting at home, eating Hula Hoops and playing a computer game?

He felt a hand in his. It was Natascha. She squeezed his hand, and whispered, "Don't be frightened."

"I'm not frightened," said Tim.

Natascha shrugged her shoulders. "I am."

Tim nodded. "Actually, I am too."

They grinned at one another.

At that moment, Max pushed past them, lifted his head and shouted to the guards, "Hey! You!" Max had an idea for what to do next. However, no one could hear him over the noise of the crowd. So Max shouted even more loudly. "Silence! SILENCE!"

No one took any notice.

Tim tapped Max on his back, and said, "I can understand what you're saying."

"So? What's wrong with that?"

"You're speaking in English."

"Good point," said Max. He shouted once more. This time, he shouted in his own language. (I shall translate the following dialogue into English.) At the top of his voice, Max shouted, "SILENCE! SILENCE!!!"

The crowd went silent. All of them looked around.

They were shocked. We are murderers, bank robbers, car thieves and tax dodgers, they were thinking. Who dares tell us to be silent? When they turned around, and saw a young boy, they were even more shocked.

In the silence, Max called up to the two guards. "You two! You guards! Can you hear me?"

One of the guards shouted down, "Yes. Why? What do you want, kiddo?"

"I shall tell you for the last time: open the gates and let us out of here."

When they heard those words, the two guards laughed. One of them shouted down to Max, "The army will be here in five minutes. If you want to stay alive, little boy, run back to your cell."

"Let us out! Open the gates!"

The guards laughed. This time, the other guard stepped forward, and shouted down, "Open them? For you? Why? Who do you think you are?"

Max drew himself up to his full height, and shouted: "My name is Max Raffifi, and I am a man of honor."

When he said those words, you might have expected a few people to snigger or giggle. Max wasn't a man; he was a boy. Compared to the massive, muscular prisoners surrounding him, he was slight and slim. However, he spoke with such dignity that no one even smiled.

Max shouted to the guards, "Do you hear me?"

The guards nodded. One of them yelled, "Go back to your cell! The army will be here in a minute!"

Max shook his head. "We aren't returning to our cells. We're going to give you a choice. This is it." He spoke loudly, slowly and clearly so everyone could hear him.

"You have two options, and only two. The first option is this. You open the gate, and let us out."

"Not a chance," shouted the guard.

Max continued. "The second option is this. We will come up there, and punish you as you deserve to be punished."

One of the guards laughed. "I think you've forgotten something." He waved his pistol. "If you come near us, we'll kill you."

The second guard shouted, "You know what? We might just shoot you now." He pointed his gun at Max.

Max smiled. He wasn't frightened. He shouted back: "How many bullets does your gun have? Six?"

The guard nodded. "That's right, kiddo."

Max continued. "You have two guns. Each gun has six bullets. Between the two of you, you have twelve shots. So, you can shoot me. And after me, you can shoot eleven more of us. You will kill twelve of us. Just twelve. But what will you do about all the rest?"

The guards didn't answer. In silence, they stared down at the large crowd of angry men, and their brows creased with worry. Below the observation tower, two or three hundred prisoners had assembled, and, every second, more hurried across the bridge to join them. Max was right. The guards might kill twelve prisoners–but what was twelve out of three hundred?

All around Max, prisoners stared at him with admiration. Three or four reached forward, and patted him on the back. He might be small, and slim, and frail, and fifteen years old. He might not know how to rob a bank or steal a car. But he had a good brain, and he knew how to use it.

Up in the observation tower, the two guards leaned their heads together, and muttered to one another. They didn't take long to make their choice. Without another word, one of them hurried to the other side of the observation tower, and pressed a red button.

The gate slid open.

With a roar of triumph, the crowd of prisoners charged forwards.

27

The three children were swept forwards by a tidal wave of men.

Each of the children was borne in a different direction. Within seconds, they had lost sight of one another. Like tiny yachts lost in a violent storm, they couldn't choose their direction; they simply let the wind carry them where it wished. They tried not to be swamped by any of the big waves, and waited to see where the tempest would drop them.

Tim felt as if he was being submerged under the sea. The water was made of arms and legs and bodies, but it still had the power to drown him. He would be squeezed, dragged under the surface and suffocated. As he saw the narrow gates approaching, he took a deep breath. He knew that the men would press together even closer as they passed through the gates.

Because the children were so much smaller than anyone else, they sank under the waves of human flesh. They lost one another. Tim looked around, trying to see the others, but he couldn't see anything. He could barely even move his head. He was crushed against one man's muscular arm, another man's thick thighs. He couldn't breathe; if he hadn't taken so much oxygen into his lungs, maybe he would have suffocated. He wasn't even walking; the sheer pressure of bodies seemed to pick him up and carry him across the ground.

His lungs hurt. They felt tight, as if they were going to burst. He desperately needed to take a breath, but he was being squeezed so tightly that he couldn't.

This is it, thought Tim. Now I'm going to die. I'm going to be crushed to death.

He tried to shout for help, but no noise seemed to come out of his mouth. He couldn't even struggle with his arms or legs, because he was being pressed so hard on every side.

I'm going to die, he thought again.

He wondered what dying would feel like. He hoped it wouldn't hurt.

At that moment, he passed through the gates.

Only a few feet away, Grk was also passing through the gates. Close to the ground, unseen by anyone, Grk squeezed through people's legs. A heavy boot trod on his paw. Grk squeaked, but no one heard him. He scuttled forward, trying to dodge through the moving forest of feet that surrounded him.

The tidal wave of prisoners surged through the gates, and emerged on the other side in an open field of yellow corn. Overhead, the sun was shining in the clear blue sky. The cornfields stretched to the horizon, swaying gently in the breeze.

Tim felt like a cork popping out of a bottle. As the crowd emerged through the gate, he was sent sprawling forwards. He staggered to stay on his feet, and pulled a deep breath of air into his aching lungs. He coughed, and spluttered, then took another long breath.

Around him, other prisoners stumbled, stopped, stood still and stared at the view. Some of them had been locked in their cells for twenty years or even more. For twenty years, they had seen the sun and the sky only through the bars of their windows. For twenty years, they hadn't looked at the natural beauty of a cornfield, swishing from side to side in the wind. They had only seen such landscapes in their dreams. Now, seeing the landscape, they were paralyzed by its beauty.

Tim noticed one man who was standing nearby.

The man was massive. He looked terrifying. If you saw him walking down the street, you would hide behind a car until he had gone past. His forearms were wider than Tim's head. Brightly colored tattoos ran along the length of his bare flesh: strange symbols sprouted on his ankles, weird words were printed on his hands and a scarlet snake curled around his neck. His face was the worst: he had a black eye, a nose which must have been broken on several different occasions and old scars scrawled all over his cheeks. To Tim's surprise, despite his scary appearance, this man was obviously transfixed by the landscape's beauty. Maybe he was a murderer, a thief or a terrorist; nevertheless, as he gazed at the cornfields and the sunlight, the man lifted his tattooed hand to his eyes, and wiped away a tear.

Tim felt someone touching his arm. He turned around. It was Natascha. She smiled. "Are you okay?"

"Fine," said Tim. "You?"

"I'm okay." Natascha nodded. "Have you see my brother?"

"No."

Both of them stared at the mass of prisoners who were still pouring through the gates. It was an extraordinary sight. Most of these men were violent, nasty and thoroughly bad–but as they stumbled through the gates and saw the landscape, a transformation occurred. Their faces lost all trace of violence or anger, and lit up with joy.

Tim said, "Why aren't they running? Don't they realize what's going to happen?"

Natascha looked at him. "What is going to happen?"

"The guards called for reinforcements, didn't they?"

"But they won't be here for hours."

"Quicker than that. Remember those jets which flew overhead? They probably called for reinforcements too. In a few minutes, hundreds of soldiers will arrive. They'll bring tanks, and guns. If these men stand here like this, they don't have a chance."

Natascha nodded, then looked at the prisoners. "So, what should they be doing?"

"They should be running as fast they can," said Tim. "And so should we."

"Aren't we going to wait for the others?"

"Of course," said Tim. "Oh, look! There's your brother!" He jumped up, and waved. "Hey! Hey! Over here!"

Beside him, Natascha screamed as loudly as she could: "Max! Max! WE'RE OVER HERE!"

On the other side of the crowd, nearer the gates, Max was pushing past a group of prisoners. He heard someone shouting his name. "Max! Max!" He stopped, and stood on tiptoes. Through a forest of heads, he could just see Tim, jumping up and down, waving his arms.

A couple of minutes later, the three of them were reunited. Only one person was still missing. "Where's Grk?" said Natascha. "Has anyone seen Grk?"

None of them had.

"He'll come soon," said Natascha. She sounded confident, but she looked worried. She pursed her lips, and whistled.

All three of them started whistling and shouting his name. "Grk! Grk! GRK! GRK!" Natascha did a special whistle which only she knew. It was three notes joined together–a high note, a low note, and another high note. Grk would have recognized that whistle; he knew that no one except Natascha whistled like that. But he didn't come running to find her.

Max said, "Let's split up. Each of us can go in different directions."

"But we've got to be quick," added Tim. "We don't have much time."

"Let's just go," said Natascha in a quiet voice.

"Go?" Max stared at her, amazed. "Without Grk?"

"If he doesn't want to come with us, he can stay here." Natascha shrugged her shoulders. "Like Tim said, if we wait any longer, we'll get caught by the soldiers. We have to go now."

Max looked worried. "What will happen to Grk?"

"He'll be okay."

Tim stared at Natascha, surprised. "Are you sure? You don't mind leaving him?"

"Of course I mind," said Natascha. "But he's found us once already, hasn't he? He'll find us again."

Tim said, "But what if . . . ?"

Natascha interrupted him. "There's something you have to know about Grk. He might be small. And he might be stupid. But he can take care of himself. Better than we can."

"Then let's go," said Tim. "The army will be here in a minute."

Tim turned round, and started pushing through the crowd. The other two followed him.

As they walked, Max put his arm around Natascha's shoulder. A look passed between them. Max whispered, "We'll find him. I promise." Max understood exactly what Natascha was doing. Natascha didn't want to risk all their lives just for Grk. So, she knew that they had to leave him behind. To save the lives of Tim and Max, she was willing to sacrifice the thing that she loved most in the world.

"He'll find us," replied Natascha. "Come on. We have to hurry."

Together, the three children ducked through the crowd of prisoners. They pushed past a forest of tattooed arms, and hurried along the road which led away from the prison.

Just beyond the prisoners, they found a patch of soft green grass, speckled with daisies. A large sign had been placed on the grass.

VILNETTA PIVLAZT SLAMT
PER FLICZT YT RECPTITAPZ
VERBADDTEN VISITATEN NABT FLIRCHT

As you probably can't read Stanislavian, I shall provide a translation:

WELCOME TO VILNETTO PRISON
PLEASE REPORT TO RECEPTION
NO VISITS WITHOUT PRIOR APPOINTMENT

The sign cast a long shadow on the grass. There, lying in the shadow, Tim and the Raffifi children saw something black and white, about the size of a folded tea cloth. It was Grk. He was taking a quick nap, using the sign's shadow to protect himself from the sun's heat. When he saw the children, his tail thumped against the ground.

Max shook his head in disgust. "That dog! He's nothing but trouble!"

"Come here," said Natascha. "Grk! Come here!" She held out her arms.

Grk sprang to his feet, and hurried to the children.

Natascha got down on the ground, and stroked his fur. "Good boy," she whispered. "Good boy."

"You shouldn't praise him," said Max. "You should scold him."

"Why?"

"Because we wasted lots of time looking for him. If you trained him better, he'd come when you whistled."

"I don't want to train him better," said Natascha. "I think he's perfect how he is."

Max shook his head. "You shouldn't be–" But no one got a chance to hear what Natascha should or shouldn't be doing, because Tim interrupted Max. "Stop arguing. Let's go."

"I'm not arguing," said Max. "I'm telling her how to look after her dog. Otherwise she'll never learn."

"Can't you tell her later?"

"What's wrong with telling her now?"

"Because we're in a hurry," explained Tim. "We have to go right now. Unless you want to be put in prison when the army arrives. Or killed."

No one wanted that to happen. So, Max stopped arguing, and Natascha stood up, and, together, the four of them continued along the road, hurrying away from the prison.

Behind them, prisoners continued streaming through the gates. Every second, the crowd grew larger.

A few of the prisoners scarpered as fast as they could, sprinting down the road or jumping into the cornfields and hiding among the tall corn. But many of the prisoners didn't move. They stood outside the prison. They stared at the sky, and the road, and the fields, and the hazy horizon. They felt the sun's warmth on their skin, and breathed the sweet air of freedom.

28

They walked in a line. Max strode purposefully at the front, keeping his eyes on the road ahead. They had made an arrangement: if Max saw a car, a tank, a soldier or any movement, he would whistle. That was a signal for the others to leap into the fields by the side of the road, and hide among the corn.

Max walked fast. The others had to hurry, or they would have been left behind. It was unfair: Max was the tallest, and, because he played football and tennis, he was the fittest. He could walk for miles without needing to rest. If they had been walking through the countryside for fun, Natascha would have complained, and forced Max to slow down. But she knew that they weren't walking for fun: they were walking to save their lives. So, she jogged after him. The sun was hot, and their clothes got unpleasantly sweaty, but no one moaned or bickered.

Natascha walked alongside Tim. She whispered, "Are we going to have to walk all the way back to London?"

"I don't know," replied Tim. "I hope not."

"Me too. How long would it take?"

"I don't know." Tim thought for a moment. "About a month, I think."

"A month!" Natascha was shocked. "I can't walk for a month."

"You'll be fine. You're stronger than you think."

Natascha nodded. "I guess you're right." She put her head down, and concentrated on walking.

Actually, Tim wasn't sure that either of them would be fine. Under the boiling sun, his thick clothes felt stifling. He took off his jumper, but he was still much too hot. Sweat poured down his forehead. His legs ached–and they had hardly started walking. Could he walk for a whole month? Definitely not. He wasn't even sure that he could walk for a whole day. Normally, he walked home from school, and no further. But he followed the example set by the others, and concentrated on walking without complaining. He tried not to think; he just put his head down, and moved one foot, then the other. One foot, then the other. One foot, then the other.

Grk's little pink tongue dangled from his mouth, and he panted. He was too hot. He was wearing a thick fur coat, but he couldn't take it off. However, Grk wasn't the type of dog who complained about things. Like his owner, he put his head down, and concentrated on walking.

A whistle came from the front.

It was Max. He had spotted some movement on the road ahead. He ducked to the left, and scrambled into the cornfields.

Tim jumped off the road. Natascha did the same. Grk scurried after them.

Seconds later, a deafening roar boomed overhead. A hundred feet above the ground, seven fighter jets flew in neat formation, heading for the prison.

As soon as the jets had gone, Max leaped to his feet. "Let's keep moving."

Natascha said, "Why don't we hide here? If we go on the road, we're more likely to meet the soldiers."

"They'll find us here."

"How?" Natascha pointed at the thick ranks of corn, which looked like an impenetrable forest. "They'd never see us in that."

"They'll have planes. And helicopters. They'll probably bring dogs too. We wouldn't have a chance. We have to find the nearest village, and hide there. The further we get from the prison, the safer we are."

Natascha nodded. "I guess you're right."

"I am right," said Max. "Let's go. Now."

Grk and the three children struggled back to the road, and started plodding along the tarmac. They were hot, tired and hungry. No one spoke.

A few minutes later, they heard a low thudding sound. It came from behind them. They stopped, and turned around. The first thud was followed by another, then several more.

Over the top of the swaying corn, they could see clouds of black smoke lifting into the air.

Natascha said, "What's that? What's happening?"

"Bombs," replied Max. "They're bombing the prisoners."

For a moment, the others were too shocked to speak. Then, Tim shook his head. "Pigs. These people are *pigs*."

"Don't talk like that," said Natascha.

"Why not?"

"Because pigs are nice."

"Pigs?" Tim was shocked. "What's nice about pigs?"

"Have you ever seen a pig? A real pig?"

Tim thought for a moment. Then, he shook his head. He had seen pigs on TV. He had seen bacon in the supermarket and pork chops on his plate. But he had never seen a real, living pig.

Natascha said, "Pigs are clean. And very intelligent. They know what it's like to be locked up. They wouldn't drop a bomb on someone just because he wanted to be free."

Tim nodded. "Yeah, okay. I'm sorry for insulting pigs."

"Don't worry," said Natascha. "None of them heard you."

"Come on," said Max. "When we get there, you can chat about animals as much as you like. Not now. Now, we have to walk."

Max started striding briskly along the road, setting the pace. The others took deep breaths, and followed him. The tarmac felt hard and uncomfortable under their weary feet, and patches of sweat blossomed on their clothes, but no one complained. They put their heads down, and concentrated on getting away from the prison as quickly as possible.

While they walked, Tim had some time to think about the Raffifi family. He found them strange. Often, he couldn't understand what they were saying, even when they spoke English rather than Stanislavian. They seemed to argue with one another all the time. (You have to remember that Tim was an only child, so he didn't understand that brothers and sisters are always arguing.) Despite their oddities, and the fact that he felt a bit scared of Max, he liked them both.

Best of all, he liked Grk. Over the past few days, he had come to think of Grk as his dog. Although he had crossed Europe to return Grk to his rightful owners, Tim had half-hoped that he might get to keep Grk. Now, he knew that he wouldn't. However, he couldn't imagine better owners for a dog than the Raffifi family.

They had been walking for fifteen or twenty minutes when Max whistled again.

He ducked to the left, and vanished into the corn. The others did the same. Except for Grk, who stood in the middle of the road, sniffing the air, looking puzzled.

As I have said many times already, Grk was not the most intelligent dog in the world.

When Natascha realized that Grk was still standing in the road, she tried to hurry back again to fetch him, but Max stopped her. He grabbed her arm, and hissed, "No! Leave him!"

Before Natascha could answer, they both heard the

sound of engines, heading along the road in their direction. Every second, the sound grew louder.

Max hissed, "Lie down! Hide! Quick!"

Natascha lay down, and whispered to her dog. "Grk! Grk! Come here! Grk!"

Grk ignored her. He stood in the middle of the road, and stared at the vehicles that were heading towards him. The engines were very loud now. It sounded as if a whole motorway was charging towards them.

As the vehicles rolled closer, Grk put his head on one side, and stared at them. He seemed to be saying: "I'm not scared of you. I'm not even worried."

With a whoosh, the convoy drove past. An APC led the way. (An APC is an Armoured Personnel Carrier; it is halfway between a car and a tank.) The APC was followed by a line of military trucks. The ground shuddered under the force of their massive wheels. Each truck carried thirty troops, armed with rifles.

Natascha gasped. Where was Grk?

Then she saw him. At the last possible moment, he had leaped out of the road. He was standing by the side of the road, watching the vehicles as they trundled past.

The final vehicle in the convoy was a black Toyota Land Cruiser containing only two men. Tim felt a great sense of relief. They had survived! Their hiding place had worked! As soon as the Toyota had driven past, they could emerge and continue along the road.

Then the Toyota stopped.

The door swung open, and a man stepped out.

29

He was a lean, bony man, dressed in a black suit. On his face, he wore a pair of black sunglasses, hiding his eyes. With a swift movement, he reached under his jacket, and removed a pistol from his shoulder holster. He pointed the pistol at Grk.

Grk put his head on one side, and stared at the pistol.

The man with the pistol cleared his throat, and spoke in a loud, clear voice. "I shall shoot this dog in five seconds."

Tim and the Raffifi children could hear what he was saying. They also recognized his voice: it was Major Raki. None of them moved. They tried not to breathe.

Major Raki said, "I know you can hear me. And I know

this is your dog. So, listen. Unless you come out from your hiding places, I shall count to five, then shoot the dog. The choice is yours. If you want to save the dog, show yourselves now." He paused, waiting for them to answer. But the only answer was silence. "Very well. After the count of five, I shall shoot him."

Major Raki took careful aim at Grk, and said, "One."

The corn swayed. No one moved. No one spoke.

"Two."

A bird flew over the field, singing loudly. Then it was gone, and the silence returned.

"Three."

Grk opened his mouth just wide enough that you could see his short, sharp, white teeth. His eyes didn't leave Major Raki's face.

"Four."

Major Raki's finger tightened on the trigger.

"Five."

Before Major Raki could shoot, a voice shattered the silence. "Stop!"

Major Raki lowered his gun, and turned to stare at the cornfields.

Natascha got to her feet. She stared at Major Raki with a defiant, angry expression. She walked towards him, brushing stray bits of corn and earth from her clothes. "Okay. You can take me back to prison."

Major Raki smiled. "And your brother? Where is he?"

"I don't know." Natascha shrugged her shoulders. "I last saw him an hour ago."

"Tell the truth, child!"

"It's true. When we left the prison, we went in different

directions. That way, you could catch one of us, but you wouldn't catch both of us."

"And the English boy?"

"I don't know. He went another way too. Like I told you, we all went in different directions."

Major Raki shook his head. He lifted his pistol, and pointed it at Grk. "If they don't come out, I kill the dog."

"But they're not here," said Natascha. "Don't you understand? They are not here."

"So, I kill the dog." Major Raki's finger tightened on the trigger.

"No!"Natascha screamed. "No! Please! No!"

"Then tell me," said Major Raki. "Where are they?"

Natascha stared at him, but she didn't speak.

Major Raki shrugged his shoulders. "You give me no choice, child." He pointed the pistol at Grk, and prepared to shoot.

At that moment, two more figures got to their feet in the cornfield. Max and Tim stood up at the same moment. Neither of them said a word. They stared at Major Raki with hatred on their faces.

Major Raki nodded. "As I thought. Come here! All of you! Quickly!" He pointed the gun at Natascha. "And don't even think about running away. This time, I shall not shoot the dog. I shall shoot her."

Max and Tim walked through the cornfield, and stepped into the road. Grk hurried to Natascha, and stood at her feet. Natascha leaned down, and tickled him behind his ears. It wasn't his fault that they had been caught; he didn't know that he had done anything wrong.

"Get in the car," said Major Raki.

Max said, "Why? Where are you taking us?"

Major Raki glanced at him. "When you get there, you will find out."

"I'd like to know now, please. Where are you taking us?"

"No more questions!" Major Raki swung open the Toyota's back door. "Get in! Now!"

Natascha and Max looked at one another. Then they looked at Major Raki's pistol. Each of them knew what the other was thinking: if they tried to fight, he would shoot them. There might be three of them, but they wouldn't have a chance. Three children and a dog couldn't defeat one ruthless man with a pistol. Natascha stepped towards the Toyota. She clambered into the backseat, and the others followed her.

Major Raki sat in the front seat, covering the children with his pistol. He wasn't taking any chances. He issued a curt order to the driver, who turned the car around, and drove back in the direction from which they had come.

They drove in silence. Tim felt scared. He clasped his hands together in his lap; if he hadn't done that, his fingers would have trembled. He was ashamed by his own fear, and didn't want the others to see how he was feeling.

To his surprise, the Raffifi children didn't look nervous. They didn't even look worried. Natascha and Max stared through the windows at the passing landscape, as if they were driving through the countryside on a sunny Sunday afternoon.

Were they pretending? Or did they really feel no fear? Tim didn't know. And, of course, he couldn't ask.

He tried to imagine some way of escaping, but it seemed impossible. Major Raki kept his gun trained on Natascha. If any of them tried to escape, or attempted to stop the car, Major Raki would kill her.

The road continued through the cornfields for a couple of miles, then joined another, larger road, which led towards Vilnetto. They passed a second convoy of military lorries, heading towards the prison. Then, the road was empty.

Max leaned forwards, and broke the silence. "Raki? That's your name, isn't it?"

Major Raki's eyes flicked at Max, then returned to Natascha. His gun didn't even waver; the barrel stayed pointed at Natascha's chest. "Yes, that is my name."

Max said, "Where are you taking us?"

"You will find out when you get there."

"I would like to know now."

"Very well." Major Raki smiled. "I am taking you to Colonel Zinfandel."

"What does he want with us?"

"You will have to ask him."

Max glanced at Natascha. Some kind of signal seemed to pass between them. Max looked at Major Raki again. "And will our parents be there?"

"Your parents?"

"Yes. Our parents. Gabriel and Maria Raffifi. When will we see them?"

"Oh, children," whispered Major Raki. His voice was quiet and cruel. "Little children. Your parents loved to talk about you, didn't they?"

Max tensed. "Have you seen them?"

"Oh, yes."

"Have you spoken to them?"

"Yes."

"What did they say? Where are they?"

"I was guarding your parents when they tried to escape."

"Escape? What do you mean, *escape*? What are you talking about?"

"A few nights ago, your parents did a foolish thing." Major Raki could see the effect that his words were having on Max and Natascha. He spoke slowly, enjoying his power over them. "They attacked a guard. Their behavior left me no choice. I killed them both."

Max was so angry that he couldn't speak. His face drained of blood. His cheeks turned the color of chalk. His hands trembled.

"He's lying," whispered Natascha. "Don't listen to him. He's lying."

Major Raki smiled. "Did no one tell you?"

Still Max did not speak. In his lap, both his hands clenched into fists.

Major Raki said, "You're not going to do anything stupid, are you?" He waggled the pistol, keeping the barrel pointed at Natascha. "Remember what would happen if you did. I shall kill your sister, just like I killed your mother and your father."

There was only one thing that Max wanted to do: he wanted to hurl himself across the car, and smash his fists into Major Raki's face. But he knew that he couldn't. He knew that his sister would be the person who suffered most.

After a long silence, Max spoke. His voice was quiet and determined. "We will not forget this."

Major Raki chuckled. "For a little boy, you take yourself very seriously."

"I am serious."

"Of course you are. And you probably think I feel scared, don't you?"

Max said, "I don't care what you feel."

"Let me tell you something, child," hissed Major Raki. "You do not scare me. And you never will."

At that moment, there was a flash of black and white. It came from the front of the car, and shot through the air. Major Raki screamed in agony, and whirled around, scrabbling at his face.

30

For the past few minutes, no one had thought about Grk. They had forgotten that he even existed. Unnoticed, Grk had been lying on the floor at Natascha's feet. He watched and listened. He waited. Then, he took his chance and moved.

Grk had a good memory. He remembered who he loved and who he hated. There was no one that he loved more than Natascha and no one that he hated more than Major Raki. For the past few days, he had been waiting for an opportunity to take his revenge.

Now, he had his opportunity.

As the car sped around a corner, he sneaked through the gap between the two front seats. No one noticed what he was doing: the driver concentrated on driving; Major Raki devoted all his attention to watching Max and Natascha; none of the children saw anything except Major Raki's face.

Grk reached the front of the car. He put his paws on the front seat, and prepared to leap. He waited for the perfect moment. His mouth opened, and all his muscles tensed.

When the perfect moment arrived, Grk leaped into the air. His jaw clamped. With one snap of his sharp white teeth, he ate a mouthful of Major Raki's face.

Major Raki had been prepared for almost anything–but he had not anticipated having his ear bitten off by a small dog.

He spun round, screaming. His finger tightened on the pistol's trigger. He fired a couple of bullets. They whizzed through the air, missed everyone and punctured the windows. Air swept into the car. The children ducked. As Major Raki twisted in his seat, trying to shake off Grk, he thumped against the driver, knocking him sideways.

"No!"

The steering wheel spun out of control. The car tumbled off the road, bounced across the grassy verge and smashed into a tree.

Metal buckled. Glass tinkled. Someone screamed. Then, there was silence.

31

No one moved. No one spoke. Time seemed to stand still.

The driver was the first person to recover. He sat up, clutching his head, and groaned. On his forehead, he could feel something wet. He touched it. Blood trickled through his fingers. He groaned again, and looked around. Seeing what had happened to the car, he didn't take more than a couple of seconds to reach a decision: he opened his door, jumped out of the car and ran away as fast as he could.

In the backseat, Natascha blinked, and sat up. She rubbed her head. Everything hurt. She looked along the seat: Max and Tim were sprawled in a heap. Natascha whispered, "Hey! Are you okay?" Neither of them replied, so she whispered louder: "Max! Timothy Malt! Can you hear me?"

One by one, they sat up. Max and Tim were dazed and shocked. They turned their heads from side to side, and wiggled their arms, checking that none of their bones was broken. Natascha said, "Are you okay?"

"Everything seems to be working," said Tim.

Max gyrated his wrists and elbows. "Me too."

Natascha said, "Where's Grk?"

"And where is . . . that man?" added Max. He couldn't bring himself to speak Major Raki's name.

They peered at the front of the car. The seats were empty, but one of the doors was open, and a man-sized hole had been smashed through the windscreen. On the splinters of broken glass, they could see some scarlet splashes which could only be blood.

"Let's get out and look," said Max.

Natascha nodded reluctantly. She was terrified of what they might find.

The three of them climbed out of the car, and walked round to the front. By the bonnet, there was a lopsided tree, which had been uprooted by the impact. A man was lying at the foot of the tree. One of his arms was twisted behind his head. His clothes were wet with blood. He didn't move.

Natascha said, "Is he . . . Is he dead?"

"Wait," replied Max. He walked quickly to Major Raki, and knelt beside him. In the collision, Major Raki's sunglasses had been smashed from his face. Now, his eyes stared blankly at the sky. His pupils were rigid. No movement disturbed his skin. Max nodded. "He's not breathing. He's dead."

"Oh," whispered Natascha. "I don't know if I'm happy or sad."

"Happy," said Max. "You should definitely be happy. There is one less evil person on the planet. That's something to be happy about."

Tim stared at Major Raki. He had never seen a dead person before. He felt a bit sick. The funny thing was, Major Raki didn't look specially dead: he looked peaceful and calm. If his clothes hadn't been soaked with blood, you would have thought that he had decided to lie in the shade under the tree and have a quick nap.

Natascha said, "Where's Grk?"

Tim and Max didn't answer. Both of them felt worried. If Major Raki had died in the crash, what would have happened to a small dog?

Natascha whistled and shouted, "Grk! Grk!" She hurried around the tree, searching. There, lying on the grass, she saw a heap of black and white fur.

She ran to him. She knelt. Grk opened his eyes, and looked up at her. He sprang to his feet, and hurled himself at her, wagging his tail as if he hadn't seen her for months.

Tim stood beside Natascha. "It's amazing. He doesn't seem to be hurt."

"It's a miracle," said Max.

Natascha didn't care *why* her dog was safe; she just cared that he was safe. She picked up Grk, and cradled him in her arms.

"Right," said Max. "What do we do now?"

"Get out of Stanislavia," said Tim. "As quickly as possible."

"And how are we going to do that?"

Natascha shrugged her shoulders. "Walk?"

"No," said Max. "It's too far. And we'd get caught. The police must be looking for us."

Tim looked at the two Raffifis. "Can either of you drive?"

"I can," replied Max. "I haven't passed my test, but I can still drive. Why?"

"We could drive to the border."

"In this car?" Max pointed at the shattered windscreen and the broken window. "We would be stopped after five minutes."

Tim said, "Maybe we could find another car."

"How? Where?"

Natascha said, "Isn't there anyone who can lend us a car? Or drive us to the border?"

"Like who?"

All of them tried to think. Max and Natascha's grandparents lived in the city, but the police would be watching their houses. Gabriel Raffifi's oldest friends had already been arrested by Colonel Zinfandel. They were silent. Until Tim said, "I know someone who might be able to help."

32

They decided that the Toyota would be usable for a short distance, even with its broken windscreen. If a policeman stopped them, they would pretend that they were taking the car to a garage.

Natascha wanted to bury Major Raki's body, or cover the corpse with some leaves, but Max insisted that they didn't have time.

(Actually, Max didn't want to dignify Major Raki's body with burial. As far as Max was concerned, Major Raki didn't even deserve to have his body eaten slowly by crows. But he knew that Natascha wouldn't agree with him–she thought that even the most evil people on the planet deserved to be forgiven for their sins–and he didn't want to get involved in a big argument with her. So he just said that they didn't have time.)

They left the body lying under the tree by the side of the road, and got into the Toyota. Max reversed back onto the road, then drove towards Vilnetto. For someone who hadn't passed his driving test, he drove with surprising skill and speed.

During the drive, several pedestrians stared at the car strangely; they had never seen a Toyota Land Cruiser with a huge hole in the windscreen, another window missing, and a fifteen-year-old boy sitting in the driver's seat. Max took no notice, and concentrated on driving. Luckily, they didn't pass any police.

In the city's outskirts, they parked the car in a residential street, and left the keys in the ignition. If anyone wanted it, they could have it. Then, the three children and Grk continued their journey on foot.

Max and Natascha had never lived in Vilnetto, because their father had always been posted to different countries around the world. However, they had spent many holidays in the city, staying with their grandparents, so they knew it well. After walking for about twenty minutes, they reached the British Embassy.

Tim said, "You wait here. I'll go alone."

"We should come with you," insisted Max. "In case you get in trouble."

Tim shook his head. "If I get caught, then you're still free. That's better. If I haven't come back in half an hour, you should leave without me. Try and get to the border."

Max couldn't argue with that. He was impressed by Tim's courage. He stuck out his hand. "Good luck."

"Thanks," said Tim.

They shook hands. Then, Tim shook hands with Natascha too, and patted Grk on the head. He felt like an explorer leaving on a dangerous journey, or a soldier going into battle. It was a good feeling.

Leaving the others, Tim walked down to the end of the road, and turned the corner. There, ahead of him, he could see the British Embassy. And there, standing by the front gate, he saw the one thing for which he hadn't planned: a policeman.

For a minute or two, Tim stood in the road, staring at the policeman, trying to think of a cunning strategy. Was there another entrance? No. Could he sneak past the policeman? No. So, what was he going to do?

Tim turned around, and walked back to Max and Natascha. Luckily, they hadn't moved. When he reached them, he asked for their help.

Throughout the day and the night, a policeman stood guard outside the British Embassy. He was bored. Nothing ever happened. So, when a little girl walked down the street and started chatting to him, he was delighted. She was a pretty little girl, about twelve years old, and she spoke beautiful Stanislavian. She smiled at the policeman. "Excuse me," she said. "My cat is stuck in a tree. Will you help me?"

"I'm sorry, little lady," replied the policeman. "I'm not allowed to leave my post."

"Please. Oh, please. It will only take one minute. And she's so scared, stuck in the tree."

The policeman looked at the little girl. "Well, where is she?"

"In the next street." She pointed round the corner, and smiled prettily at the policeman. "Just there."

"I don't know," said the policeman. "It's strictly against the rules."

"Please. Oh, please."

"All right. But I'll have to be quick. You're sure it won't take more than a minute?"

"I'm absolutely sure."

"Come on, then."

"Thank you so much," said the little girl, and led the policeman along the street.

As soon as the policeman turned his back, a shadowy figure slipped through the entrance into the British Embassy.

Together, the policeman and the little girl walked around the corner until they reached a gate. "Wait here," said the little girl. "I'll go and get the key."

"Which key?"

"For the garden. Wait here." The girl smiled, and hurried away.

The policeman didn't exactly understand what was going on, but she seemed a nice, polite girl. So he stood in the street and waited.

Five minutes later, he was still waiting, but the little girl never returned.

• • •

When the policeman's back was turned, Tim slipped through the entrance, and hurried across the gravel path towards the British Embassy.

He ducked behind the hedge, and crept along the wall. Above him, he could see the outlines of windows. If he bent double, he could pad along the gravel below the level of the windows. No one would see him.

He stood up, and slowly, carefully, eased his head around so he could see through one of the windows. Big oil paintings glared down from the walls. At a table, beside a massive computer, two men in black suits were arguing. Tim ducked down before they noticed him.

He crept along the gravel to the next window, and peered through the glass. Inside the room, he saw a maid. She was wearing a black uniform and a white apron. With a pink feather duster, she was dusting the furniture. As she turned towards the window, Tim ducked, and hurried onwards.

He came to a third window. It was open, so he could hear what was happening inside. He heard a woman's voice. He crouched under the windowsill, and listened. "There's a full-scale riot," the woman was saying. "We have reports of five hundred troops. Maybe even more." Then she paused. After a few seconds, she continued: "Not since he was seen leaving in the helicopter, no."

Either the woman was talking to herself, or she was speaking on the phone. Tim stood up straight, and peeked through the window.

On the other side of the glass, he saw a small room, crowded with filing cabinets and books. A large desk was covered with sheets of paper. The room's occupant was sitting with her back to him, talking on the telephone. Although Tim couldn't see her face, he recognized her voice. She was the person that he had come to find.

Slowly, he slid his fingers under the window. Gently, he lifted it. Inch by inch, he raised the window.

Inside the room, the woman continued talking on the phone. "That's a mystery to me too, sir."

When the window was half open, Tim lifted his leg over the sill, and clambered into the room. He managed to make no noise. He tiptoed across the room.

The woman laughed. She said, "Of course I will. As soon as I hear anything." She put down the receiver, turned around to pick up a file and saw Tim. She jumped. Her mouth dropped. Then she laughed. "You're very quiet. You'd make a good thief, wouldn't you?"

Tim shrugged his shoulders, and grinned. "I'd rather be a spy."

"Well, Her Majesty's Government is always looking for volunteers."

"Okay," said Tim. "I'll volunteer."

"Maybe when you're a little older." Miranda leaned back in her chair. "Do you realize, Tim, how much trouble you've caused?"

"No. How much?"

"A lot. Thousands of people are searching the country, looking for you. The British papers are going mad. You're the first item on the TV news. The Prime Minister is being kept informed. And Colonel Zinfandel . . . Well, let's just say he's not a happy man."

Tim giggled.

"It's not funny," snapped Miranda. "This is extremely serious."

"I know," said Tim. "Sorry."

"Right." Miranda stood up. "Let's go and find Sir Cuthbert."

"We can't."

"What do you mean?"

"We can't tell him what's going on."

"Why not?"

Tim explained what had been happening since he and Miranda had last seen one another. He described the planes bombing the prison, the convoy of troops and how Major Raki's body had come to be lying under a tree by the side of the road. He explained about the Raffifi children, and their parents. "They have to get out of the country. Otherwise, Colonel Zinfandel will kill them."

"You don't know that."

"Yes, I do," insisted Tim. "If he finds them, he'll kill them. He will, won't he?"

Miranda bit her lip, and nodded.

Tim said, "There's only one person who can help them."

"And who's that?"

Tim looked at her, but he didn't say a word.

Miranda understood immediately what he meant. "Oh, no." She shook her head. "Not me. Not a chance."

"Please, Miranda. Please. Otherwise, Max and Natascha are going to die. Please, Miranda. We have to stop Colonel Zinfandel killing them. Don't we?"

Miranda stared at Tim for a long time. She seemed to be considering a lot of things. She bit her lip, and looked around the room, and bit her lip some more. Finally, she nodded.

Tim started thanking her, but Miranda put up her hand to stop him. "You can thank me tomorrow. If we're not in prison. Or dead. Until then, don't bother thanking me. We've got too much to do. All right?"

"All right," said Tim.

"Good. Let's get moving."

Miranda worked fast. She hurried around her room, collecting what she needed: her passport, her purse, a few clothes, some papers and three large gray bags. Each of the bags had black letters printed on the side: DIPLOMATIC BAG—PROPERTY OF HER MAJESTY'S GOVERNMENT. Tim wanted to ask what the bags were for, and why Miranda needed them, but he remembered what she had said about not talking. So he kept quiet.

When Miranda had stuffed her clothes and possessions into a leather satchel, she picked up the telephone, and dialed a number. She had a short conversation which went something like this:

"Hello? Sir Cuthbert?"

In his private office, Sir Cuthbert answered the phone. "Yes? Yes? Who's that?"

"Sir Cuthbert, it's Miranda."

"Good! Now, I want to know everything! What's happening? Have you made any progress?"

"We've just received a call from a possible witness. A young English boy has been seen in a village about ten miles from here."

"Jolly good! Terrific! Great news! Let's go!"

"Perhaps I should go alone."

"No, no. I want to come too. I'll meet you on the front lawn in two minutes."

"There's only one problem, Sir Cuthbert. What if the Foreign Secretary rings back? Do you think someone should stay here to take his call?"

"The Foreign Secretary," repeated Sir Cuthbert. "Yes, yes. Good thinking, Miranda. I'll stay here, and speak to him. You'll keep me informed, won't you?"

"I certainly shall, Sir Cuthbert." Miranda put the phone down, and winked at Tim. "Let's go. Where are your friends?"

"Hiding in the next street."

"Can you climb out of the window again?"

"Sure," said Tim.

"Good. Do that. And take this." Miranda handed the bag to Tim. "Wait outside. I'll pick you up in the car."

Miranda hurried out of the room, locking the door after her. When she had gone, Tim dropped the bag through the open window, and jumped after it. His feet crunched on the gravel; he hoped no one would hear the noise. He squatted on the ground, holding the bag, and waited.

After a few minutes, he heard the noise of tires. A black Range Rover rolled around the corner. Miranda was driving. She beckoned to Tim. He sprinted across the gravel and clambered into the back of the Range Rover, carrying Miranda's satchel.

"Get down on the floor," ordered Miranda.

Tim crouched down where he couldn't be seen. Miranda drove out of the Embassy, and waved to the grumpy policeman who was guarding the gate. He didn't wave back. Miranda accelerated along the street. "Now which way? Where are they?"

"First left," said Tim from his hiding place.

They took the first left, then stopped halfway down the road. Tim opened the door, and checked that the street was empty. When he was sure that no one could see him, he did the whistle that he had learned from Natascha: a high note, then a low note, then another high note. Almost immediately, the hedge quivered, and three disheveled figures emerged. The Raffifi children brushed the loose leaves from their clothes and ran towards the Range Rover. Grk shook himself, and trotted after them. They clambered inside the car, and sat on the backseat.

Miranda turned to look at them. She grinned. "Hi. I'm Miranda. You don't have to introduce yourselves, because I know who you are. At the Embassy, we've already received faxes of your photographs, describing you as violent and dangerous criminals. There's a large reward for your capture."

"How large?" asked Max.

"Ten thousand dollars."

Max whistled. "Ten thousand? That's not bad. Maybe we should give ourselves up, and claim the reward." Max looked at the others. "What do you think?"

"I've got a better idea," said Natascha. "Let's hand you over. Then, we'd still get half the reward, and we wouldn't have to put up with you all the time."

"Ha, ha," said Max. "Very funny."

Natascha pretended not to hear him. She looked at

Grk. "What do you think, Grk? How many bones could we buy for five thousand dollars?"

Tim stared at Max and Natascha, astonished by their calm. How could they make jokes at a time like this? How could they be so cheerful when their lives were in danger? They were weird, he decided. But they were also quite cool. He wished that, like them, he could smile and joke when faced with death.

"Let's get moving," said Miranda. "They'll be setting up roadblocks soon. Everyone ready?"

They all nodded.

"Hold tight." Miranda put her foot down. The tires squealed, and the Range Rover accelerated along the road.

33

Stanislavia is a landlocked country. That means it has no borders touching the sea. However, its borders do touch several other countries, so you can sneak in and out of Stanislavia along many different roads. Each border crossing has a customs post, guarded by soldiers who check your passport and inspect your car to make sure that you're not smuggling any guns, drugs, cheap cigarettes or illegal bottles of brandy.

Miranda drove towards one of the smallest border crossings, high in the mountains that ring the north of the country. There, she hoped, the guards would be dozy, so they wouldn't bother examining the car properly.

They drove out of the city, and joined the road that

went north. A large sign announced that the border was three hundred kilometers away. Tim, Max and Natascha slumped down in their seats so they couldn't be seen from other cars. Grk lay on the floor at Natascha's feet.

As they drove, the landscape changed. First, the city gave way to fields. Then, the fields merged into long valleys, punctuated by small, sleepy villages. On the horizon, they saw hazy mountains, tipped with snow.

When they had driven for a couple of hours, Miranda's mobile phone rang. She answered it. "Hello?"

"Miranda!" Sir Cuthbert's voice echoed fuzzily through the phone. "You've been gone for two hours! Where are you?"

"I'm stuck in a traffic jam."

"Have you found that boy?"

"No, sir."

"No? No? What do you mean, no?"

"I mean I haven't found him, sir."

"That's not good enough," spluttered Sir Cuthbert. "Come back here this minute!"

"Yes, sir."

"And when I say this minute, I mean this minute!"

"Yes, sir."

"If you're not in my office within ten minutes, I'll . . . I'll . . ."

"Yes, sir?"

"I'll be jolly cross."

"Very good, sir. I'll see you in ten minutes." Miranda ended the call. As an afterthought, she switched off her phone.

Tim looked at her. "Won't you get in trouble?"

"For what?"

"For disobeying Sir Cuthbert."

"Oh, I'll get into all sorts of trouble," said Miranda. She tapped her fingers on the steering wheel. "I'll probably get fired. No, no, that's not true. I'll definitely get fired."

They drove for another two hours. The landscape changed again, becoming more rugged and less hospitable. They drove into the Northern Stanislavian mountains, where few people live. On both sides of the motorway, thick forests covered the hillsides. Buzzards hovered overhead.

This is one of the few places in Europe where wolves still roam in the wild. Every spring, shepherds lose one or two of their lambs to the wolves. Every autumn, hunters come from the city to kill a wolf. They are rich men with big guns. All of them want a nice soft wolf-skin to hang on their walls and show off to their friends.

Sometimes, the rich men shoot a rabbit or a pigeon, but they never even catch sight of the wolves. The wolves are too clever for them. Every year, the rich men return to the city empty-handed, humbled by the mountains and the forests.

As the road climbed higher, the air grew chilly. Miranda switched on the car's heating, but the children still shivered. Natascha pulled Grk off the floor, and laid him on her lap, trying to borrow some of his warmth.

Twenty kilometers before the border, they passed a big hand-painted sign:

LAST CHANCE TO BUY PETROL IN STANISLAVIA. WE SELL GOOD COFFEE TOO, AND HOME-COOKED SNACKS.

A couple of minutes later, they reached the garage. Miranda stopped to buy a full tank of petrol. The home-cooked snacks had sold out, but she bought eight bars of chocolate and a two-liter bottle of water.

At the next turning after the garage, Miranda pulled off the road, and kept driving until she found a little lane, hidden from sight by some trees. She parked the car. They got out. Miranda handed round the chocolate–two bars each–and everyone gulped down some water.

Natascha cupped her hands to make a bowl. Max poured water into it for Grk to drink. When Grk lapped the water out of her hands, Natascha giggled. "That tickles. Stop it! That tickles!" Grk took no notice, and kept licking her hands. He was thirsty.

Tim said, "You know the problem with eating? It just makes you realize how hungry you are."

"The border shouldn't be more than fifteen or twenty minutes from here," said Miranda. "On the other side, we'll stop for supper. Okay? And I'm buying."

Max asked, "Won't they be waiting for us?"

"Who?"

"Soldiers. The police. Customs. On the border. Won't they have our photographs?"

"Probably," replied Miranda.

"And we don't have our passports," added Natascha. "Even if they don't recognize us, they won't let us through."

"It'll be fine," said Miranda.

"How do you know?"

Without another word, Miranda walked round to the back of the Range Rover, and fetched her leather satchel.

She unzipped it, and pulled out the three gray bags that she had taken from her office. Each of them was printed with the following words: DIPLOMATIC BAG—PROPERTY OF HER MAJESTY'S GOVERNMENT.

Miranda showed the bags to Max and Natascha. "You grew up in an embassy, didn't you? So you must know what these are."

"Yes, of course," replied Max.

"Explain them to Tim. He doesn't."

Max looked at Tim. "A diplomatic bag cannot be opened by anyone. You use it to send things to people in your embassy."

Tim asked, "What type of things?"

"Whatever you like. Passports. Bottles of whiskey. Presents. Only people from the embassy are permitted to open the diplomatic bag. It's private, and secret."

"No one can look inside a diplomatic bag," added Miranda. "Not soldiers. Not customs officials. Not even the police. Anything inside a diplomatic bag is protected. As you'll have noticed, these bags are particularly big." Miranda lifted one of the bags; it was as tall as her. "Big enough for a person."

The children stared at her. Max said, "That's crazy."

"Do you have a better suggestion?"

Max thought for a moment, then shook his head.

Natascha pointed at Grk. "What about him?"

"You'll have to share. Come on, climb in." Miranda opened the three bags, and placed them on the ground. They were like long, thin sleeping bags. One by one, the three children clambered inside. Natascha called Grk. He sprang across the ground, and leaped inside her bag too.

Miranda opened the Range Rover's boot, and said, "Now you have to get in here."

Like contestants in a sack race, the three children bounded across the ground to the car.

"It's going to be a tight fit," said Miranda. "But you won't be inside for very long. Sorry, but I'll have to tie you up. I hope none of you suffers from claustrophobia."

Miranda fetched a roll of yellow tape. She pulled the loose material over the tops of the bags, and tied them up. Then, the children wiggled into the Range Rover's boot, and lay down, squeezed together. If you had glanced into the boot, you would have seen three gray bags. You might have guessed that they were stuffed with letters or clothes or important official documents. You would never have suspected that they contained three children and a dog.

Miranda said, "Everyone okay?"

Three muffled voices answered.

"Yes." (That was Max.)

"Yes, thanks." (That was Tim.)

"We're fine." (That was Natascha, who was answering for herself and Grk.)

"Good," said Miranda. "See you on the other side of the border." She slammed the door, and locked it. Then she got into the driving seat, started the car, turned around and drove back to the main road.

Inside the dark, hot, sweaty bag, Natascha clasped Grk to her. She tickled his ears, and whispered to him: "Don't worry. We'll get out soon."

Grk wriggled round, and licked her face.

"Ugh." Natascha wiped her face with her hand. "Don't do that."

But he did it again.

Inside the second bag, Max closed his eyes and dreamed that he was dribbling.

The goalie passed the ball to him, and he dribbled it out of his half. He nutmegged their center-forward, and passed it to someone who passed it straight back again. Max took the ball to the edge of the penalty area, and lobbed it to one of his teammates, who knocked it round one of the fullbacks, and delivered a short pass to Max.

In slow motion, he saw the ball spinning towards him. He twisted his body, and launched a fierce kick, powering the ball towards the net. The goalie dived, his fingers outstretched.

The goalie's fingers brushed the ball, but it wasn't enough. Max's shot was too strong. The ball plunged into the back of the net.

The crowd roared. Max was surrounded by his teammates. Out of the corner of his eye, he could see the dejected goalie picking the ball from the back of the net.

Inside the third bag, Tim felt terrified. He thought he was going to die. He couldn't breathe. He was hot. Sweat dripped down his skin. He closed his eyes, and tried to pretend that he was somewhere else. Anywhere else. But where?

He thought for a minute or two; then he had an idea.

He imagined that he was lying in a tent on the side of

Everest. A storm was raging outside the tent. Snow piled against the side of the tent. Wind battered the walls. Ice formed in every gap and crevice. That was why Tim was curled inside a dark, sweaty sleeping bag: to keep out the cold.

Tomorrow, he and his fellow mountaineers would make an assault on the summit. They would climb the highest peak on the planet.

Tim had once seen a TV documentary about climbing Everest. He tried to remember all the details of the landscape and the complicated equipment that the climbers had used.

Miranda tried not to think about the three children, confined to bags in the car's boot. What if they suffocated? What if they sneezed? What if one of the border guards decided to poke the bags with a bayonet? She tried to put those questions out of her mind, and concentrated on the road.

After twenty minutes, the Range Rover arrived at the border. It was marked by a tall fence, about twice the height of a man. Red and white striped barriers prevented cars entering or leaving the country.

Very few people used this border. If you wanted to enter or leave Stanislavia, you would usually take one of the quicker roads which didn't wind through the mountains. At this border post, the soldiers rarely saw visitors. They spent their days watching TV, playing cards, polishing their boots and cleaning their guns.

As the Range Rover drove toward the border crossing, a lazy soldier lifted himself out of his deck chair, and picked up his rifle. He yawned. He was a tall, handsome man with a big mustache. His name was Corporal Yoran Lilas. He had been born in the North of Stanislavia, and had never lived anywhere else. He had never wanted to.

I should let you know a few facts about the inhabitants of Northern Stanislavia. They are proud, and fiercely independent. They are hunters and shepherds. They love the mountains and the forests. There is one thing that they hate: being told what to do.

Over the centuries, the inhabitants of the North have gained a reputation for being lazy. If you hire one of them, people say, he won't work hard. He will take two days to finish a job that would be completed by anyone else in an afternoon. When your back is turned, he will lie down in the sunshine, and take a quick nap.

But the Northern Stanislavians aren't really lazy. They just don't like being told what to do. They don't like working for other people. If they are working for themselves, they work as hard as anyone in the world.

Corporal Lilas stuck out his arm, gesturing for the Range Rover to stop.

Miranda braked. The Range Rover rolled to a halt beside the soldier.

Corporal Lilas knew immediately that Miranda was a foreigner, because the Range Rover had a special numberplate to show that it belonged to the British Embassy. He held out his hand. "Passport!"

Miranda handed over her passport. Corporal Lilas opened it, and looked at her picture. Then he looked at her, and winked. "You look better in real life."

"Thanks." Miranda smiled.

Corporal Lilas handed back her passport, and walked around the car. He looked in the boot. He saw the three bags. "What is in here?"

"Diplomatic bags," said Miranda.

"Open them, please."

"No."

Corporal Lilas stared at her, astounded by her refusal.

Miranda explained, "I don't have to open diplomatic bags."

"Yes. You must. Open them."

"No. They are diplomatic bags. You're not allowed to search them."

"I am allowed to do anything," said Corporal Lilas. "I am Stanislavian Army."

"I don't care who you are," replied Miranda. "You can't open a diplomatic bag."

Corporal Lilas was irritated. He didn't like anyone telling him what to do. He hadn't specially wanted to open the bags until Miranda told him that he couldn't. That changed his mind. Now, he was determined to see the contents of all three bags. He switched on his radio, and called for reinforcements.

Two more soldiers emerged from the hut, wiping soup from their mustaches. They had been eating–and nothing annoyed them more than having their meal interrupted. They hurried down the hill, carrying their rifles. When they reached the Range Rover, Corporal Lilas explained the situation. The three soldiers peered through the Range Rover's window, staring at the diplomatic bags in the boot, and discussed what to do.

• • •

Inside the bags, the children could hear voices. They knew that the car had stopped. They realized that Miranda had reached the border. Only a few more minutes, and they would be safe. Only a few more meters, and they would cross the border into freedom.

Inside the first bag, Tim lay very still. He bit his bottom lip with his upper teeth, and stared through the thick woolen lining of the sack. He wanted this to be finished as quickly as possible. He closed his eyes and tried to retreat back into his daydream. . . .

He was climbing Everest. Behind him, he could see the mountainside stretching for miles. Ahead, through the swirling cloud, he saw the peak of the world's tallest mountain. A few more steps, he told himself. One foot after the other. Plodding through the snow. And he would reach the top. He would be the youngest person ever to climb Everest.

Inside the second bag, Max forgot his imaginary game of football, and made a plan for defending himself. He flexed his fingers, tensed his muscles and prepared to fight. Even if they had guns, he was going to fight. He would rather die here than spend the rest of his life in one of Colonel Zinfandel's prisons.

Inside the third bag, Grk was getting restless. He didn't like lying down inside this dark, hot bag. And, even worse, he needed a pee.

"Shhh," whispered Natascha as quietly as she could. "Stay still, Grk. Stay still."

Grk tried to stay still, but he couldn't. He was desperate

to pee. His bladder was bursting. He started wriggling, trying to find a way out of the bag. So Natascha grabbed him, and held him tightly against her body.

Corporal Lilas noticed some movement inside one of the bags. He tapped on the glass, and shouted at Miranda. "What is in there?"

"Where?"

"In that bag." He pointed at the gray bag which had wriggled. "What is it?"

Miranda said, "None of your business. As I said, diplomatic bags are not your concern."

"Yes, it is my business. Tell me."

"No."

"Yes! Tell me! I am police here!"

"But I am a British diplomat," explained Miranda. "Those bags contain items of diplomatic importance. By the rules of international law, you are expressly forbidden from opening diplomatic bags."

The soldiers looked at one another. They didn't entirely understand what Miranda had said. That made them even more suspicious, and even more irritated. They had a muttered conversation. All of them wanted to open the bags. One of them wanted to shoot Miranda, but the others persuaded him not to.

They finished their discussion. Corporal Lilas said to Miranda, "We open bags. Now. Unlock the car."

"You can't do that," said Miranda.

"Yes," said Corporal Lilas. "Now!" At that moment, all three soldiers raised their rifles, and pointed them at Miranda.

Confronted by the barrels of three rifles, Miranda realized that she had no choice. She walked round to the back of the car, and unlocked the boot.

One of the soldiers lifted the boot. Corporal Lilas produced a knife. He slit the tape at the top of the bag, and opened it.

Then he stumbled back, shocked, as a small dog poked its head through the hole.

The dog was followed by Natascha. She tried to hold Grk, but he wriggled out of her arms, and jumped out of the Range Rover.

Grk landed on the ground, bounded across the grass and sprinted to the nearest tree. There, he lifted one of his back legs, and had a long, satisfying pee.

A minute later, the three soldiers were inspecting their catch: a small dog, a British diplomat and three children.

As soon as Max and Natascha Raffifi emerged from the bags, the soldiers recognized them. That morning, a fax had arrived from the Ministry of Information. At the top of the fax, two grainy black-and-white photographs showed the Raffifi children. The rest of the fax explained these two children were dangerous fugitives. They were guilty of several serious crimes. They were dangerous, and probably armed. A ten-thousand-dollar reward would be given to anyone who captured them.

Miranda glanced at the three children, and silently mouthed one word. "Sorry." The Raffifi children smiled back at her. They knew that Miranda had done her best.

One of the soldiers said, "Ten thousand dollars. Not bad, huh?"

The second soldier shook his head. "It's not not bad. It's fantastic. If I did this job every day for the rest of my life, I wouldn't be able to save up ten thousand dollars."

Corporal Lilas said, "We divide it between us, right?"

"Sure. We divide it three ways."

"So, how much is that each?"

The three soldiers thought for a minute or two. None of them was very good at maths. They rubbed their heads and moved their lips while they counted.

Finally, Natascha got so impatient that she told them the answer. "It's three thousand, three hundred and thirty-three dollars each. And thirty-three cents."

The soldiers stared at her. "Really?"

"Yes," said Natascha. "Really."

Corporal Lilas whistled. "Three thousand dollars!"

The second soldier said, "Three thousand, three hundred and thirty-three dollars! And thirty-three cents!"

The third soldier said, "What are you going to do with it? Save or spend?"

"Spend," said Corporal Lilas. "I'll buy a new car. You?"

"Take my wife on holiday. We haven't been on holiday for five years."

"Where will you go?"

"I don't know." The soldier shrugged his shoulders. "Maybe Florida. She's always wanted to go there."

"I'd like you to remember who we are," interrupted Miranda. "I am an employee of the British Government. This boy"–she gestured at Tim–"is a British citizen. You have no right to hold us against our will."

"Go, then," said Corporal Lilas. "You can go. Cross the

border. We don't care about you. We just want them." He pointed at the two Raffifi children.

"Why? For the money?"

"That's right," said Corporal Lilas. He grinned. "Ten thousand dollars? I'd sell my mother for that."

The second soldier said, "Who would buy your mother for ten thousand dollars?"

"That's not the point."

"Then, what is the point?"

"The point is this," said Corporal Lilas. "I would be prepared to do anything for ten thousand dollars."

A new voice entered the conversation: "Even betray your own country?"

The three soldiers turned around, shocked and surprised, to see who had spoken those words.

It was Max.

Corporal Lilas said, "You're the traitor."

"No, I'm not," said Max.

"You are," insisted Corporal Lilas. "You're a traitor or a criminal. That's why there's a reward for your capture. And you must be a serious criminal, otherwise the reward wouldn't be so big."

Max smiled. "Do I look like a criminal?"

When none of the soldiers replied, Max pointed at Natascha. "Does my sister look like a criminal?"

Still, none of the soldiers replied. Corporal Lilas stared at the ground. The other two soldiers looked a bit embarrassed. Finally, Corporal Lilas lifted his head and looked at Max. "Okay, you don't look like criminals. But we're soldiers. We don't judge people by their appearances. And, for all we know, you might be dangerous terrorists. You might be plotting to destroy our country."

"There's only one person who is going to destroy Stanislavia," said Max. "And his name is Colonel Zinfandel."

The three soldiers looked nervous. They glanced around, checking that no one could hear what was being said.

Max didn't care who heard him. "We are not criminals," he insisted. "We're enemies of Colonel Zinfandel, that's all. We hate him."

"Shhh," hissed one of the soldiers. "The trees have ears."

"He has spies everywhere," explained another soldier.

"I don't care," said Max. "I won't keep quiet. I hate Colonel Zinfandel, and I hate what he has done to our country. If you were true citizens of Stanislavia, you would hate him too."

Corporal Lilas whispered, "Maybe you're right. Maybe Colonel Zinfandel isn't such a great guy. But what can we do? We're just three poor soldiers."

"You can let us go," said Max. "That will hurt Colonel Zinfandel. It might not hurt him very much, but it will hurt him a little. The only way to overthrow a dictator is hurting him again and again, little by little, until his power is destroyed."

The three soldiers looked at one another. None of them knew what to do. They hated Colonel Zinfandel, as did many people in Stanislavia. The people in the North hated him more than anyone else, because he kept telling them what to do. However, they were terrified of him. They didn't want to be tortured by his secret police. They didn't want to be locked in prison or forced to work in the salt mines. Even worse, they knew that Colonel Zinfandel wouldn't just punish them: he would punish their families, their wives, their children, even their dogs.

Corporal Lilas said, "How do we know that you're not one of his spies?"

"You have to trust us," said Max.

The soldiers looked at one another again. In low voices, they whispered to one another. They waved their arms and argued angrily.

"We have to arrest them," said the second soldier. "We have to! If we don't, Colonel Zinfandel will kill us. And not just us. He'll destroy our families. He'll burn down our houses. He'll make us wish that we'd never been born."

"We have to arrest them," said the first soldier. "We have to! Think of the money. Ten thousand dollars! Once in their lives, everyone gets a chance like this. A chance to make some serious money. This is the only chance we'll ever have."

"We have to let them go," said Corporal Lilas.

"Why?"

"What are you talking about?"

"There are only two reasons for arresting these children," explained Corporal Lilas. "The first reason is greed. The second reason is fear. Are those good reasons for doing anything?"

The other two soldiers looked at him for a long time. They thought about the money, and imagined what each of them could do with three thousand, three hundred and thirty-three dollars. They thought about Colonel Zinfandel, and imagined what would happen if he discovered that they had freed the Raffifi children. In their minds, they saw firing squads, and burning houses, and prison cells, filled with their families. Then, at the same moment, they both shrugged their shoulders, and nodded.

Corporal Lilas turned around and looked at Max. He spoke for all of them. "Go. Now. Before anyone sees you."

"Thank you," said Max. "We will not forget this."

"Thank you, thank you," said Natascha.

"Go," repeated Corporal Lilas. "Before we change our minds."

Tim, Max, Natascha and Grk leaped into the back of the car. Miranda climbed into the front, and started the engine. She waved to the soldiers, but none of them waved back.

The barrier lifted. As the Range Rover drove across the border, leaving Stanislavia behind, the soldiers watched it for a second.

"There goes ten thousand dollars," said the first soldier.

"Ten thousand dollars," muttered the second soldier. "Ten. Thousand. Dollars."

"Forget it," said Corporal Lilas. "Just forget it. Forget you ever saw them. Okay? Because if Colonel Zinfandel ever discovers what we've done . . ."

He didn't need to finish his sentence. The other two soldiers nodded. All three of them turned their backs on the Range Rover, and tried to wipe it from their mind.

On the other side of the border, there was another checkpoint. It belonged to a different country, so the soldiers wore a different uniform. One of them looked at the Range Rover's diplomatic plates, glanced through the window at Miranda and three children, and waved the car onwards.

Miranda drove through the border, and kept driving until they passed a restaurant. There, they stopped for a quick supper. After eating lamb stew and cucumber salad, followed by pancakes with walnut syrup, they continued to the nearest airport, where Miranda used her credit card to buy five tickets on the first plane to London.

While they were waiting for the plane to board, Miranda made two phone calls to tell people when the plane would arrive in London. First, she rang Tim's parents. Second, she rang the Foreign Office.

On her voice mail, Miranda had eleven messages. Every one of them had been left by Sir Cuthbert. "You can't still be stuck in traffic," said his eleventh message. "Where are you? *Where are you?* If you don't call me back in ten minutes, I shall have to . . . I shall . . . I'll . . . I'll . . . Well, you'd better call me back, that's all I can say."

Miranda switched off her phone, and didn't bother calling Sir Cuthbert.

A few hours later, Tim, Max, Natascha and Miranda walked through Customs at Heathrow Airport. Grk had already left the airport by a different exit, for reasons that will be explained in the next chapter.

As the four of them emerged through the gates into the Arrivals Hall, they were met by an extraordinary sight.

A hundred cameras pointed at the children. Someone had tipped off the press, and told them that Timothy Malt would be returning to Britain on this flight.

With a mighty whirr, the cameras recorded the scene.

Flashes popped, illuminating the children's faces with a pale light. Microphones dipped down to catch every word from their lips–but none of them made a sound, because they were too shocked to speak.

A hundred journalists shouted a hundred questions at exactly the same time: "Tim! Timothy Malt! Over here, Tim! How does it feel to be home again? Tell us what happened! Where have you been? Over here! Are you glad to be home? Smile for the camera! Timothy Malt! Tim! Over here!"

It was shocking. For a moment, Tim was so disorientated that he didn't understand what was happening. He blinked. His eyes went fuzzy. He felt confused and lost. When he saw two people running towards him with their arms outstretched, he felt scared. Who were they? What did they want? What were they going to do to him? Then he recognized them.

"Oh, Tim," said his mother as she wrapped her arms around him. "You're safe! You're safe!"

Tim looked up at his father, who was standing above him. They grinned at one another. There was no need for words.

34

When you bring an animal into Britain, you have to lock him in a cage for six months. This is called quarantine. According to the government, quarantine is necessary to protect British animals from the foul diseases that only exist in foreign countries. During those six months, vets will regularly inspect your pet, and check that he doesn't have rabies, ticks, tapeworm or any other unspeakable infections.

Smart animals avoid quarantine by having special pet passports. Grk had one too. Unfortunately, he had left the country without it, so he had to go straight into quarantine on his return. When Tim, Miranda and the Raffifis arrived at Heathrow Airport, the British customs officials arrested Grk and took him into custody.

They didn't snap handcuffs around his paws, but they did lock him in a little cage. Grk's ears drooped. He peered through the bars at Natascha, and he wrinkled up his nose. His expression seemed to be saying, "I came and rescued you from prison–and this is how you repay me? By putting me in prison?"

Natascha knelt beside the cage and tried to apologize. Grk wasn't impressed. He turned his back on her and lay down in the corner of the cage, sulking.

That afternoon, Mr. Malt made several phone calls, and found a kennels just outside London, less than an hour's drive from the house. The owners agreed to take Grk, and give him a home for the next six months.

The kennels was a dog prison–no one could deny that–but it was a comfortable dog prison. During his imprisonment, Grk lived in a large cage. He always got two long walks, one in the morning and one in the afternoon. He was given a constant supply of water, tennis balls and chewy toys. Best of all, he was visited almost every day by Tim and the Raffifis.

As for Max and Natascha, they came to live in London. Mr. and Mrs. Malt invited them to stay, and they gratefully accepted. Mr. Malt moved his books and his computer out of the attic, and converted it into a bedroom. Natascha slept there. Tim shared his bedroom with Max. The house felt cramped, but no one minded.

At Tim's school, the headmaster agreed to take two extra pupils. Every morning, Tim, Max and Natascha walked to school. Every evening, they walked home together. Never again did Tim have to walk home alone, and let himself into an empty house.

• • •

One afternoon, about a fortnight after he had returned to London, Tim climbed the stairs to the attic. He knocked on the door. A voice came from inside the room: "Yes? Who is it?"

"Me," said Tim.

"Who's me?"

"Me. Tim."

The door opened. Natascha grinned. "You don't have to knock. It is your house."

"It's your house too now."

"Is it?"

"Yes."

"Oh. Okay." Natascha grinned again. "Well, would you like to come into my bedroom?"

"Yes, please."

Tim followed Natascha into the attic. In the past fortnight, the room had changed completely. Mr. Malt's desk and computer had been replaced by a bed and a long pole with lots of hangers to hang clothes. At the moment, most of the hangers were empty; Natascha only owned a few items of clothing. Next weekend, she and Mrs. Malt had made a date to go shopping in Oxford Street. On the shelves, where Mr. Malt used to keep his boring insurance books, Natascha had placed a few novels, a map of London, three books about dogs and an English–Stanislavian dictionary.

Tim said, "Miranda just rang. She's coming round tonight for supper."

"Oh, good," said Natascha. "What happened with the Foreign Office? Did she get fired?"

Tim shook his head, and explained. According to Miranda,

Sir Cuthbert had sent a stream of angry e-mails and faxes to the Foreign Secretary, demanding that Miranda was sacked immediately. Finally, the Foreign Secretary sent a letter back again, telling Sir Cuthbert that Miranda had been promoted to reward her for her good work, and she might even receive a medal. The Prime Minister had sent a personal message to congratulate Miranda for helping Tim and the Raffifis.

Natascha clapped her hands gleefully. "That's such good news! That's great news! So, what's she going to do now?"

"She's going to America," said Tim. "To work in the Embassy there."

While they were talking, Tim had noticed three things pinned to the white wall above Natascha's bed.

First, there was a photograph of Grk. He was staring at the camera. His head was tipped on one side, and his ears were perked up as if he was listening to some distant music.

Second, there was a sheet of white paper. Tim crossed the room to look at it. On the paper, Natascha had written eight English words in capital letters:

TEMPEST
GRAMOPHONE
AZURE
DRAKE
WITNESS
HADDOCK
FIDDLE
MAGNET

Tim pointed at the paper. "What's this?"

"My words."

"Which words?"

"Every night, I learn eight words. For improving my English."

"How do you choose the words?"

Natascha shrugged. "From the newspaper. Or hearing people in the street. Or on the bus. Overhearing them. No, no, no. Eavesdropping them. Is that right? I eavesdropped them on the bus. That's right, isn't it?"

"Yes, I think so," said Tim. Actually, he wasn't quite sure. It didn't sound quite right, but it didn't sound entirely wrong either. He looked at the list again. "What's a drake?"

"You're English, and you don't know?"

"I'm only twelve."

"So am I. And I'm not even English." Natascha grinned. "Maybe you should learn eight words a day too."

Tim wasn't amused. "Are you going to tell me what it means, or do I have to look it up in the dictionary?"

"Of course I'll tell you. It's a kind of duck. A male duck."

"Okay."

"Actually, I wanted to ask you. If a male duck is called a drake, what is the word for a female duck?"

"Don't ask me," said Tim. "Ask my dad. He knows stuff like that." Tim looked at the third thing pinned to the wall. It was a calendar. All the days until yesterday had been crossed out with a red pen. "And what's that?"

"For Grk."

"What do you mean?"

"To tell when he comes home." Natascha flicked through the pages of the calendar. Five months into the future, a date had been circled. "There. That's when he comes out." With a red pen, she had drawn a big circle around the date of Grk's release.

"I've got an idea," said Tim. "On that day, shall we have a party? To celebrate."

Natascha nodded. "A party would be nice. And, you know what? I'm going to buy him the biggest bone he's ever seen."

Every night for the next five and a half months, last thing before going to sleep, Natascha crossed off one more date on the calendar. Finally, six long months after Grk had gone into the kennels, he was released.

The Malts threw a big party. All their friends and neighbors came. Everyone was eager to meet this dog that they had been told so much about.

Natascha went to the local butcher, and got a huge bone. At the party, she gave it to Grk. The bone was twice as long as him, but he still managed to pick it up and grip it between his teeth. He retreated to the end of the garden, where he dug a hole, uprooting Mrs. Malt's geraniums, and buried the bone under a layer of fine soil. Then he walked three times in a circle on the flower bed, lay down and fell asleep.

After that, Grk, Natascha, Max and the Malts lived happily ever after.

35

Actually, that is not quite true. Max and Natascha were happy, yes, but their happiness was always plagued by anger, pain and fear. The two Raffifi children could never be truly happy, because they could never forget what had happened to their mother and father. Nor could they ever forget what had happened to their country.

Every day, Max remembered the promise that he had made to his parents.

He had stood in the courtyard of Vilnetto Prison, and made a solemn promise that he would rescue them. Well, he didn't. He couldn't. When he made that promise, they had already been killed by Major Raki.

In London, he made another promise. In his mind, he spoke the following words to his parents:

"I'm sorry that I couldn't help you. I'm sorry that I wasn't there when you died. But I promise you this: I shall take revenge for your deaths. And I promise, Mother and Father, my revenge will be swift and cruel."

One day, Max would have the chance to fulfil his promise. He and Natascha Raffifi would return to Stanislavia with Grk and Tim. Together, the four of them would take revenge for the murders of Mr. and Mrs. Raffifi, and liberate the country from Colonel Zinfandel.

But that's another story.

An Interview with Joshua Doder

by Josh Lacey

I arranged to meet Joshua Doder on the top of Primrose Hill, one of the nicest parks in London. I had hoped that he would bring a dog–perhaps even one called Grk–but he was alone. We stood there for a few minutes, staring at the sights of London, then strolled slowly down the hill and found a quiet café. Doder ordered a cappuccino and an almond croissant. I began by asking a few questions about Grk.

JOSH LACEY: If Grk was here, what do you think he'd have to say for himself?

JOSHUA DODER: He probably wouldn't say anything. He'd just stare at my croissant with big hungry eyes and make me feel so guilty that I'd tear it in two and give him half.

JL: What breed is he?

JD: I'm not sure. You'd have to ask him.

JL: Is he based on a real dog?

JD: No, but I did meet a dog in Podgorica who, I think, inspired me to write about Grk.

JL: Podgorica? Where's that?

JD: It's the capital of Montenegro.

JL: And where exactly is Montenegro?

JD: It's a small country on the Adriatic coast, bordered by Croatia, Bosnia, Albania and Serbia. The name Montenegro means "black mountain." It's a wonderful place. Beautiful scenery. Fascinating people. And delicious food. If you ever go there, make sure you eat roast lamb.

JL: I will, thank you. So what were you doing in Podgorica? Were you on holiday?

JD: My wife was working there and I went to visit her. One day, a friend of hers found a thin white dog in the street.

JL: How did she find it?

JD: Him.

JL: Sorry, him. How did she find him?

JD: She was just driving through the city. At a crossroads, she saw a group of people standing in a circle, abusing a dog. They were kicking him. And spitting on him. Really disgusting behavior. My wife's friend stopped her car, jumped out and started shouting at these people, telling them to leave the dog alone.

JL: That was a brave thing to do.

JD: Brave, and a little bit foolish. These were bad people. They didn't like being told what to do. Especially by a woman.

JL: What did they say to her? Did they try to justify their behavior?

JD: No, they didn't say anything. She didn't give them time. She just grabbed the dog. Picked him up in her arms. The people were so surprised, they didn't even try to stop her. She put the dog in her car and drove away.

JL: How did the dog react?

JD: I think he was as surprised as everyone else. To be honest, I have a feeling that my wife's friend was quite surprised too. She just reacted without thinking. Anyway, when she got home, she had a look at the dog. He didn't have a collar. Or a tag. She talked to the police, but no one had reported a missing dog. She couldn't find his owner. Maybe he never even had an owner.

JL: What do you mean?

JD: He might have been born on the streets. Maybe he managed to survive by scavenging. Stealing food from dustbins. Eating whatever he could find.

JL: What was he like? How would you describe his personality?

JD: He was crazy. Tense. Anxious. Manic. Unable to sit still. Always jumping around, searching for food, watching out for danger. He was like a very nervous soldier, always waiting for the next attack.

JL: You weren't tempted to adopt him?

JD: No, no. But I did find him completely fascinating. As soon as I saw him, and heard his story, I wanted to know more about him. There were so many questions that I would have liked to ask him.

JL: Such as?

JD: Where was he born? What happened to his mother? How did he spend the days and nights that he lived alone on the streets? Had he dodged traffic? What did he eat? How did he live? What did he see? Grk is a very different kind of dog in just about every way, but he was inspired by that Montenegrin runaway.

JL: What has happened to that dog now?

JD: She still owns him. The same woman, my wife's friend. She kept him. And he's still crazy, although not as crazy as he was.

JL: Do you have a dog yourself?

JD: My wife and I used to have a borzoi. A Russian wolfhound. A huge beast. He was strong, stubborn and extremely mischievous. Sadly, he died about a year ago. We then took care of another dog for a friend, but he hated strangers, and growled and barked at anyone that he didn't recognize. As we live in a busy part of London, he was constantly unhappy. He's now gone to live in Snowdonia, in North Wales, and he's much happier there.

JL: Do you have any other pets?

JD: I've been traveling a lot recently, so I haven't wanted to get another dog or any other pets. Right now, we only have one animal in the house, a very small mouse who lives in the kitchen and comes out at night. He's fearless. He squats near the bin and watches us while we're having supper.

JL: Does he have a name?

JD: I'm sure he does, but I don't know what it is.

JL: And where have you been traveling?

JD: Most recently, I went to Brazil, researching another book about Tim and Grk.

JL: Brazil? That's an interesting choice of location. Why did you pick Brazil?

JD: Because I've been there several times and I love it.

JL: And what happens to Tim and Grk?

JD: You'll have to read the book to find out.

JL: Oh, come on. Do they go dancing in Rio? Do they sail down the Amazon?

JD: I'm not going to tell you.

JL: Do they meet Pelé? Or the girl from Ipanema?

JD: There's no point trying to guess. I'm really not going to tell you.

JL: Please.

JD: No.

JL: Oh, please. Just give us a hint.

With a sigh, Joshua Doder reached into his jacket.

JD: I suppose you could read this.

JL: What is it?

Without saying a word, Joshua Doder pulled a few sheets of crumpled paper from his pocket. He handed them to me. I spread them on the table and started reading.

When I lifted my eyes, I was alone. Joshua Doder had gone.

Looking around the busy street, I couldn't see any sign of him. I waited for a few minutes, hoping he was visiting the toilet or a nearby shop, but he didn't reappear.

I paid for our cappuccinos and croissants, and walked slowly home, carrying a few pages from his next novel.

Here are those pages. . . .

Don't miss Grk's next adventure!

Turn the page for an excerpt from Joshua Doder's

Grk and the Pelotti Gang

Available from Delacorte Press in December 2007

PUBLISHED BY DELACORTE PRESS
AN IMPRINT OF RANDOM HOUSE CHILDREN'S BOOKS
A DIVISION OF RANDOM HOUSE, INC.
NEW YORK

ORIGINALLY PUBLISHED IN THE UNITED KINGDOM IN 2006
BY ANDERSEN PRESS LIMITED

A week later, on the other side of Rio de Janeiro, three men walked into a bank. They ordered everyone to lie on the floor, then forced the manager to open the vault and stuffed five brown sacks with cash. That time, the Pelotti gang got away with ninety-seven million *reais.*

Three days after that, the Pelottis robbed another bank in Rio. They stole eighty-eight million *reais,* six bags of diamonds, nine gold ingots and the salami sandwich that the bank manager had been planning to have for lunch.

Six days after that, they went back to the Banco do Brasil, and robbed it again. That time, they got away with a hundred and four million *reais.*

If this carried on for much longer, there wouldn't be

any money left in Brazil. The Pelotti brothers would have it all.

Someone had to stop them.

But who?

● ● ●

A zombie lurched through the tunnels. Flesh dripped from its rotting face.

The zombie opened its mouth, exposing two brown teeth and a throbbing red tongue. In a low, rumbling voice, it groaned, "Are you ready to die?"

Timothy Malt stared into the zombie's bloodred eyes and said, "No."

The zombie chuckled. Its mouth opened even wider. It whispered again, "Are you ready to die?"

"I said no," replied Tim. He pressed a button. Three high-velocity bullets fizzed from the barrel of his rifle and thumped into the middle of the zombie's chest.

"Die!" screeched the zombie in a terrifying, high-pitched voice. "You must die!"

"Actually," replied Tim, "I think you must die." He pulled the trigger again and again. The zombie screamed, toppled over and lay on the ground, not moving.

Tim grinned. He pressed SAVE so he wouldn't have to go back to the beginning of the level if another zombie got him. Then he stepped over the zombie's body and sprinted down the dark tunnel.

Grk lifted his head. His nostrils twitched.

Grk was lying on the floor in the sitting room, not far from Tim's feet. He had been lying there for about an hour, not quite asleep, but not quite awake either. The screams of zombies didn't disturb him. He could happily doze through the roar of grenade launchers and the crackle of bullets. But now, for the first time in an hour, his ears pricked up.

Without removing his eyes from the screen, Tim said, "What is it?"

Grk didn't answer. But he sprang to his feet, ran to the window and jumped onto a chair that gave a good view of the road. When Grk looked through the window and saw who was outside, his tail thumped on the chair's seat.

"Who is it?" said Tim.

Although he knew very well that Grk couldn't speak, he hadn't got out of the habit of talking to him. Tim had the strange sense that Grk could always understand just about anything that was said to him.

Grk barked. *Grrrrwf!*

If Tim had been able to speak Dog, he would have known the meaning of the word "Grrrrwf!" Unfortunately, Tim could only speak English, a little French and a few words of Stanislavian.

Tim pressed PAUSE on the control and ambled over to the window. Through the glass, he could see a thin fifteen-year-old boy walking towards the house. The boy was wearing white shorts and a white T-shirt, and carrying a tennis racket.

Grk barked again, louder. *Grrrrrrrrrrwff!*

Hearing him, the boy looked up and waved. Tim waved back and Grk barked again.

"Come on," said Tim. "Let's open the door."

As Tim and Grk walked to the front door, Tim wondered

whether Grk had psychic powers. Was he telepathic? Could he see the future? If not, how did he always know when someone was going to arrive at the house? Why did he always lift his head and prick up his ears a few seconds before the doorbell rang?

Tim opened the door, and said, "Hi, Max. How was practice?"

"Fine, thanks," said Max, and walked into the house. He slotted his tennis racket into the umbrella stand, then turned round. "I have a key, you know."

"I know."

"So you don't have to let me in. I could let myself in."

"I know," said Tim.

"So you must like letting me in?"

Tim nodded. "I suppose I must."

"Fine," said Max. "I'm going to have a shower. See you later."

Max ran up the stairs, taking them two at a time. Tim and Grk ambled back into the sitting room. Tim sat on the sofa, pressed a button on the control to start the action and returned to killing zombies. Grk sniffed the carpet, walked round in a circle three times and lay down.

Apart from Tim, Max and Grk, three other people lived in the house: Mr. Malt, Mrs. Malt and Natascha Raffifi. Mr. and Mrs. Malt were Tim's parents. Both of them were working. Natascha Raffifi was Max's sister. This afternoon, just like every afternoon, she was sitting in her bedroom, reading a newspaper.

Other people read newspapers in the morning, but Natascha didn't have time. In the mornings, she was rushing from her bedroom to the bathroom, showering and dressing and cleaning her teeth. Then she was rushing downstairs, eating breakfast and putting on her shoes and going to school. She couldn't imagine how anyone could possibly have time to read a newspaper in the morning.

Natascha read the newspaper later in the day, when she came home from school. She collected the newspaper from the kitchen table, where it had been left by Mr. or Mrs. Malt, and carried it upstairs to her bedroom. She sat on the bed. She collected her notebook and her dictionary. She spent an hour, and sometimes more, reading the newspaper slowly and carefully from beginning to end, stopping whenever she found a word that she couldn't understood. She looked up all the difficult words in the dictionary, and wrote them down in her notebook.

Today, for instance, the front page said, "Peace plans in jeopardy after bombing."

Jeopardy.

Natascha stared at that word for a long time. It looked a bit like "leopard" and a bit like "jealousy," but neither of those would make any sense in the context.

She shook her head, and looked up "jeopardy." According to the dictionary, "jeopardy" meant "the risk of loss, harm or death." Natascha wrote down the word and its meaning in her notebook.

In the months that she had been living with the Malts, Natascha had filled seven notebooks. They sat in a row on the bookshelf above her bed. She didn't just write down the new English words that she had learned. She jotted down interesting thoughts that occurred to her, and funny things that other people said, and good bits that she read in books. If she met someone who fascinated her, or did something unusual, or had a particular thought that she didn't want to forget, she wrote that down too. When Natascha grew up, she was going to be a writer, although she hadn't yet decided exactly what kind of writer. A playwright, perhaps. Or a journalist. Or perhaps even a poet.

But she wasn't planning to grow up for a long time. For now, she just wanted to learn lots of interesting new English words.

She hunched over the newspaper, and read the business pages, and the sports pages, and the arts pages, and the home news, and the foreign news. At the bottom of the page marked "International News," she saw a small paragraph with a surprising headline.

She read the headline, then read the whole paragraph.

Her face went white.

She read the paragraph again, checking that she hadn't imagined it. Then she read it again to check that she hadn't misunderstood any of the English words. Then she grabbed the newspaper, jumped off the bed and ran through the house, shouting, "Max! Max!"

There was no answer.

She shouted louder: "Maaaaaaaaaax!"

There was still no answer.

She ran downstairs and charged into the sitting room. Tim was squatting on the sofa, staring at the TV.

Natascha said, "Where's Max?"

Without looking up from the TV, Tim said, "Shower."

"Thank you." Natascha ran upstairs again, and tried to open the bathroom door. It was locked. She could hear the sound of running water coming from the other side. She hammered on the door. "Max? Max? Are you in there?"

There was a pause; then a muffled voice said, "What do you want?"

"Open the door."

"I'm in the shower," said the muffled voice.

"Then get out."

"Why?"

"Because I have to show you something," said Natascha.

"Can't it wait for five minutes?"

"No."

"Just wait. I'll be out in five minutes."

"Come on, Max. Open the door. It's important."

"It had better be," said the muffled voice.

Natascha waited impatiently, listening to the sounds coming from the other side. She heard water being turned off, and footsteps, and someone grumbling to himself.

The door opened. Max Raffifi looked at his sister with an impatient glare. He had a white towel tied around his waist. Water was dripping from his body to the floor, forming a small pool at his feet. He said, "So?"

"Look," said Natascha. She thrust the newspaper at her brother. "Read that."

"You got me out of the shower to read the newspaper?"

"Yes."

"I'll read it later," said Max. He tried to shut the door–but he couldn't, because Natascha put her foot in the way. "Read it," she insisted, thrusting the newspaper at her brother.

"You're very annoying," said Max. He took the paper. His wet fingers left dark marks on the newsprint. "What am I supposed to be reading?"

"That," said Natascha, pointing at a paragraph at the bottom of the page marked "International News."

Max glanced at the paragraph. He read the headline. He blinked, and leaned forwards, and read the headline again. He whispered, "I don't believe it."

Max retreated into the bathroom, carrying the newspaper, and sat on the edge of the bath. He read the whole paragraph, then read it twice more. Natascha stood in the doorway, watching him.

When Max had finished reading the paragraph for the third time, he lifted his head and looked at Natascha. He said, "What are we going to do?"

JOSHUA DODER was born in 1968. He has worked as a journalist and a teacher. He lives in London.